MYTHS AND LEGENDS

THE KNIGHTS OF THE ROUND TABLE

DANIEL MERSEY
ILLUSTRATED BY ALAN LATHWELL

First published in Great Britain in 2015 by Osprey Publishing,
Kemp House, Chawley Park, Cumnor Hill, Oxford, OX2 9PH, UK
4301 21st. St., Suite 220, Long Island City, NY 11101, USA
E-mail: info@ospreypublishing.com

Osprey Publishing is part of the Osprey Group

A CIP catalog record for this book is available from the British Library

Print ISBN: 978 1 4728 0616 1
PDF e-book ISBN: 978 1 4728 0617 8
EPUB e-book ISBN: 978 1 4728 0618 5

Typeset in Garamond Pro and Myriad Pro

Originated by PDQ Media, Bungay, UK
Printed in China through Worldprint Ltd

15 16 17 18 19 10 9 8 7 6 5 4 3 2 1

Osprey Publishing is supporting the Woodland Trust, the UK's leading woodland conservation charity, by funding the dedication of trees.

www.ospreypublishing.com

Contents

Introduction

In a magical, timeless land named Logres – now known as the British Isles – the brave Knights of the Round Table served Arthur, the great king of legend and folklore. Questing far and wide across the land, these armoured warriors upheld the king's chivalric values, righted wrongs, and maintained law and order. Together these knights formed the Order of the Round Table: an elite band of warriors from Logres and overseas.

The Round Table symbolized Arthur's desire for equality and fairness: although the knights seated at the table were proud and privileged warriors serving a powerful king, there was no head or foot of the table and therefore it lacked hierarchy and symbolized something other than the feudal system of lords and vassals. The 12th century writer Robert Wace explained that Arthur used this table to placate the nobles who served him, as none would agree to sit at a humbler place than his peers. The number of knights seated at the Round Table varies according to storyteller; most often 150 or 300 seats were at the table, although Robert de Boron placed just 50 knights around it and Layamon claimed 1,600 (at what would presumably be the world's largest piece of furniture). Arthur's Round Table was located at his court and castle of Camelot. Its first written appearance in Arthurian legend was in Wace's *Roman de Brut* (completed 1155), which was an adaptation of Geoffrey of Monmouth's earlier *Historia Regum Britanniae*. Wace noted that the Round Table was not his own invention, but originated in an earlier tale from Brittany.

Some of Arthur's knights had weaknesses and on occasion they would fail dramatically, yet none lacked bravery. Many of the stories about Arthur's knights highlight the perils of ill-chosen action as much as they celebrate good deeds, and as such they informed a real-life code of honour for medieval nobles and set the standards by which chivalry was to be judged.

Although King Arthur was introduced as a key character in medieval literature by Geoffrey of Monmouth in the early 12th century, the most influential works about Arthur's knights were written by Chrétien de Troyes later in the same century, and by Sir Thomas Malory in the 15th century. Many other deeds of the Round Table evolved across Europe and although the origins sit squarely in medieval England and France, adventures from other countries are interweaved and popular embellishments were made by 19th- and 20th-century authors. My own retellings are inspired by sources as varied as modern films and Victorian children's books in addition to the original

Lancelot slays a dragon; many of Arthur's knights fought and overcame such creatures including Yvain and Tristan. By Arthur Rackham from Alfred W Pollard's *The Romance of King Arthur and his Knights of the Round Table* (1910). (Alamy)

medieval stories: every writer of Arthurian lore adds their own ornamentation. Inevitably the narrative in a book of this length cannot furnish each story in its entirety: a bibliography of scholarly and at times challenging works of medieval and later literature which tell the whole story may be found at the end of this book.

The chapters in this book describe a diverse selection of the adventures of Arthur's knights from his coronation, through his ascendancy, and up to the appearance of the Holy Grail. Many of the later deeds of the Knights of the Round Table are far darker and relate to the arduous quest for the Grail and the eventual downfall of Arthur. As a consequence, the Grail Quest's most famous knights – including Galahad, Perceval, and Bors – are not principal characters in this book. Arthur's rise to power and kingship, alongside his place in Celtic folklore and post-Roman British history are covered in my companion volume (*Myths & Legends 4: King Arthur*).

The Knights of the Round Table have evolved into an integral part of Western culture, remaining popular in fields so diverse as stories for children, as the setting for television series and movies, and as a building block of modern fantasy roleplaying and computer games. The legend of Arthur and his knights lives on and reinvents itself for new audiences time and time again.

An Arthurian Literary Timeline

Stories of the Knights of the Round Table were told first by English and French writers between the 12th and 15th centuries; even today, most books of Arthurian fiction draw inspiration from these and are little changed from the originals. Below is a list of some of the most influential works of Arthurian legend dating back to the 12th century AD.

1130s Geoffrey of Monmouth: *Historia Regum Britanniae*
1150s Robert Wace: *Roman de Brut*
Geoffrey of Monmouth: *Vita Merlini*
1160s Chrétien de Troyes: *Érec et Énide*
1170s Chrétien de Troyes: *Yvain: Le Chevalier au Lion*
Chrétien de Troyes: *Le Chevalier de la Charrette*
Chrétien de Troyes: *Cligés*
Marie de France: *Lanval*
1180s Chrétien de Troyes: *Perceval: Le Conte du Graal*
Renaut de Beaujeu: *Le Bel Inconnu*
Hartmann von Aue: *Erek*
1190s Layamon: *Brut*
Ulrich von Zatzikhoven: *Lanzelet*
Béroul: *Tristran*
1200s Hartmann von Aue: *Iwein*
Robert de Boron: *Perceval*
Robert de Boron: *Merlin*
Wolfram von Eschenbach: *Parzifal*
1210s *Lancelot du Lac*
Queste del Saint Graal
1220s *Estoire de Merlin*
Estoire del Saint Graal
1230s *Mort Artu*
Suite du Merlin
1240s *Le Roman de Tristan de Léonis*
1380s *Sir Gawain and the Green Knight*
1390s *Alliterative Morte Arthure*
The Awntyrs of Arthure
1400s *The Avowing of King Arthur*
1450s *The Wedding of Sir Gawain and Lady Ragnell*
Gest of Sir Gawain
1470s Sir Thomas Malory: *Le Morte Darthur*
1480s Print edition of *Le Morte Darthur*
1590s Edmund Spenser: *The Faerie Queen*
1690s John Dryden: *King Arthur The British Worthy*
1800s Walter Scott: *Sir Tristrem*
1830s Alfred Tennyson: *The Lady of Shalott*
1850s Alfred Tennyson: *Idylls of the King*
Matthew Arnold: *Tristram and Iseult*
1860s Richard Wagner: *Tristan und Isolde*
1880s Richard Wagner: *Parsifal*
Mark Twain: *A Connecticut Yankee in the Court of King Arthur*
Sidney Lanier: *The Boy's King Arthur*
1900s Howard Pyle: *The Story of King Arthur and His Knights*

Prologue: The Order of the Round Table

In the old days of Logres, those days of knights and dragons, the Britons fought between themselves in a bloody civil war. The many and petty kings of the island each desired the title of Pendragon: the High King.

A noble named Uther eventually hacked a clear path to become Pendragon with the help of the powerful wizard Merlin; after Uther's death a boy named Arthur was revealed as his secret son, the boy proving his right to rule by pulling a magical sword from a stone. King Arthur fought many battles to secure his throne, gathering a growing band of loyal knights to fight alongside him. When the wars were won, Arthur proved to be an honourable and fair ruler and yet more knights and kings flocked to his castle of Camelot to serve him.

When Arthur married his graceful queen Guinevere, the wedding present from her father King Leodegrance was the Round Table. This oaken slab symbolized the democracy that Arthur staunchly upheld: no knight would sit at the head of this table – not even the king himself – and every seat was of equal worth.

Around this table at the royal court of Camelot, Arthur gathered his most loyal and skilful warriors; at this emblematic table, alongside Guinevere and Merlin, Arthur acted in the best interests of his people and his realm, seeking advice and receiving support from those seated with him. These knights became members of Arthur's Order of the Round Table, dedicated to upholding his laws and acting with honour and chivalry above all other desires.

Arthur urged his warriors to venture out on quests to right wrongs, defeat fantastical monsters, and defend the kingdom… armed with shield and lance, war-horse and armour, they became known as The Knights of the Round Table.

The First Quest of the Round Table

The marriage of King Arthur Pendragon and Guinevere was a grand spectacle attended by the great and good of all Logres. Arthur's knights were in high spirits as the king knighted more young warriors on his wedding day: among them were Arthur's nephew Gawain and Tor, the son of Arthur's ally King Pellinor. The people of Camelot were equally joyous, wonder spreading at the beauty and grace that was Guinevere. Even Merlin, sorcerer to the king, was in fair mood as he revealed the wedding gift from Guinevere's father: a huge oaken round table around which Arthur could seat his knights and set them off to adventure. It stood in the Great Hall at Camelot, sunlight gleaming from the polished surface, empty seats waiting to be filled by Arthur's followers.

The wedding feast was splendid: imported wines and exotic fruits, game from the forests surrounding Camelot, and a lake's worth of fish were laid out for all to share. As the guests took their places, Arthur announced that someone must tell a tale of wonder before the feast commenced. Merlin told the king to wait but a short while for his request to be fulfilled.

From outside came sounds of commotion and into the hall crashed a white hart, racing a jaw's-length ahead of a white hound and 60 black hounds. The hart circled the hall several times, sending fine wine and food tumbling from the tables onto the flagstones; everywhere the hart dodged the hounds followed, snapping as they went. Bitten by the white hound and desperate to pull free, the hart leaped fully over the head of a seated knight named Abelleus, disappearing from the feast almost as quickly as it had arrived. As the white hound made to follow, Abelleus swept it up into his arms and ran from the hall carrying the barking bundle with him, the black hounds following behind.

As the wedding guests picked themselves up, and removed food from their clothing and hair, a lady rode into the hall shouting at Arthur. Halting before him, she exclaimed that the white hound was hers, and begged Arthur to send a knight to fetch it back. As she spoke, yet another rider appeared amid the chaos of the upturned feast, a fully armoured knight unknown at Camelot. He seized the bridle of the mounted lady's horse, and swept away with her.

Arthur's laughter broke the silence; his tale of wonder had begun. Merlin rebuked him for taking these events too lightly… for this, the sorcerer foresaw, was the first quest of the Round Table and to fail would bring dishonour to the king. These words spurred Arthur into action. He called upon Gawain to bring back the white hart, Tor to fetch the white hound, and King Pellinor to return with the kidnapped lady. These three knights donned their armour, armed themselves, and rode from Camelot in pursuit of adventure.

Gawain rode with his brother Gaheris, who acted as his squire; with them ran a pack of hounds intent on picking up the hart's trail. This they did and Gawain and Gaheris set off into the forest beyond Camelot in pursuit of their quarry. For a full day they gave chase, and with the hart in sight they followed into the courtyard of a castle standing in a boggy forest clearing. The hart was cornered and Gawain's hounds brought it down, killing it before he could call them off.

As Gawain stooped to cut the hart's head off to prove to Arthur that he had pursued and found it, a challenge rang out across the courtyard. The lord of the castle was running towards him, huge sword in hand and bristling with fury. Shouting at Gawain that the hart was his, he cut down the hunting dogs as they stood over its white carcass. Gawain was furious to see his hounds slain, and he set about the lord with his sword.

The two warriors' blades clashed and echoed around the courtyard, and sparks flew as metal ground against metal. Gaheris ran to aid his brother but before he could land a blow, Gawain had knocked the sword from his enemy's hand and, forgetting his knightly vows in his anger, raised his blade high to deliver a killing stroke. Another voice cried out: this time, it was the lady of the castle begging for Gawain's mercy. She ran across the courtyard trying to protect her fallen lover from the intruders. Too late, Gawain realized what was happening but could not stop the deathblow from falling: the lady was between his blade and his target, and her head rolled from her shoulders. The lord begged Gawain to kill him also for he loved his lady and now had no reason to live.

In John Boorman's brooding film *Excalibur* (1981), the newly crowned Arthur (Nigel Terry) and Lancelot (Nicholas Clay) duel, leading to the Lady of the Lake gifting Arthur his magical sword Excalibur. Medieval legend ascribed this duel to Pellinor and Arthur. (Alamy)

Gaheris restrained his brother and reminded him that a knight must be merciful. Gawain sheathed his sword and sent the injured lord, Ablamor of the Marsh, to tell Arthur of his defeat by the knight who quested after the white hart. This he did.

With the castle to themselves, Gawain and Gaheris rested after their arduous day. As they sat, four knights appeared and accused Gawain of shaming all warriors of knighthood, suddenly attacking both brothers. Exhausted and unprepared, Gawain and Gaheris were knocked to the ground and one of the knights shot an arrow into Gawain's arm. Were it not for the timely arrival of four fair ladies, the knights would have slain Arthur's knights, but the ladies begged for mercy and persuaded Gawain and Gaheris to yield as prisoners.

As one of the ladies tended to Gawain's injured arm, she asked his name. He explained that he was a nephew of Arthur's and was undertaking a quest for the great king. When the lady realized his bond to Arthur, she angrily told him that slaying a lady was a foul deed, made worse because Gawain served an honourable king. She instructed him to return to his king and be judged.

The four knights stood aside as their prisoners slowly rode from the castle, Gaheris carrying the head of the hart to show to Arthur. Around Gawain's neck hung the head of the lady of the castle, and her body lay across his saddle. This sorry procession returned to Camelot.

When Tor rode from Camelot in pursuit of the white hound, he headed in a different direction to Gawain. Riding hard, he soon came upon a dwarf standing on the pathway. Tor did not slow his horse, such was his concern with his quest, until the dwarf cracked a heavy wooden club across the nose of Tor's horse. It reared up, almost throwing Tor from his saddle.

The dwarf gestured towards a nearby pavilion, by which a rogue knight waited on a charger. Tor explained that he had not the time to accept any challenge other than returning with the white hound for Arthur. The dwarf shrugged and gestured once again, calmly highlighting to Tor that the knight was now bearing down upon him at full speed, lance levelled.

Merlin

Merlin was the greatest sorcerer or wise man that Logres ever knew. Introduced to the Arthurian cycle by Geoffrey of Monmouth in his *Historia Regum Britanniae*, the king and his wizard quickly became inseparable in British legend. By Malory's *Le Morte Darthur*, Merlin helps Arthur's father Uther to seduce Arthur's mother Igraine, arranges for the future king's fostering with the good knight Ector, and sets in action the vignette of the Sword in the Stone where Arthur takes the crown. Once Arthur is ensconced as Pendragon, Merlin flits in and out of the adventures and is eventually imprisoned by Vivien (the Lady of the Lake).

In some versions, Merlin himself creates the Round Table and makes the names of knights magically appear on the seats. His character has been linked to one or more pseudo-historical northern British bards in the post-Roman period, but the medieval Merlin is better recognized as the blueprint for many wizards in more modern literature.

King Arthur and Palamedes joust, from the 15th-century *Roman du Saint Graal*. Palamedes replaced Pellinor in later legend as the hunter of the Questing Beast. (Alamy)

The duel was short but brutal. Lances split on shields, sword blades rung together, and in a few moments, the bellicose knight lay on the ground surrendering his weapon to Tor. As he did so, a second felonious knight rushed at Tor. Tor parried the first attack on his shield and before his new assailant could recover, smote his helmet with an almighty blow that rendered him senseless but living. This second knight also surrendered. Tor triumphantly commanded both knights to journey to Camelot and report to Arthur that they were prisoners of the knight who quested after the white hound. The knights, Felot of Langduk and Petipace of Winchelsea, did as they were told and served Arthur loyally from that day on despite their previous misdeeds.

The dwarf stepped up as Tor remounted his horse, telling the knight that he knew of his quest and could take him to the hound. His payment, he said, would be to become the knight's servant rather than continuing in the service of such rogues. Tor agreed and the dwarf led on.

Arriving before a brilliant white pavilion standing beside a priory, the dwarf announced to Tor that the hound would be found inside. Tor dismounted and approached the tent; lifting the flap he saw four ladies sleeping, and at the feet of the most distinguished of the ladies lay the very white hound he searched for. As it saw him, the hound leapt to its feet and started to bark.

Tor grabbed the hound and bundled it into the arms of his dwarf at the very same time as the ladies awoke. He hastily explained that he had been instructed to fetch the dog by his king, Arthur, and rode away quickly with the hound across the dwarf's saddle.

A short distance away, a knight blocked their path. It was Abelleus, the knight who had dashed from the wedding feast carrying the dog. Abelleus approached, shouting for Tor to yield and return the hound to the white pavilion. Tor refused.

The two knights charged at one another. Both were thrown from their saddle at the crunching impact of lance on shield. They arose lightly and drew their swords as eagerly as lions, hammering each other in a duel that raged for many hours. Finally, Abelleus' battered helmet fell to the ground and its owner fell with it. Tor stood over him, deciding what to do next.

In that brief lull, an unknown lady rode up. She begged Tor to grant her one wish: the head of Abelleus, who had cut down her brother in murderously cold blood.

Abelleus struggled to his feet, threw down his sword, and attempted to run from Tor. Without thinking and with the lady's request in his mind, Tor wildly swung his sword at his fleeing foe and cleaved his head into two parts. The lady thanked him, and Tor, his dwarf, and the white hound continued their journey back to Camelot.

Pellinor left Camelot at the same time as Tor and Gawain. So eager was he to fetch the kidnapped lady back to Arthur that he vowed that nothing would distract him. Riding through the forest beyond Camelot, he passed a lady sitting under a tree, cradling a dead knight in her arms. She wept miserably and cried out for help, but he did not tarry as she was not the lady he had been asked to rescue.

Riding on, Pellinor entered a valley. There stood two pavilions, and outside them fought two knights on foot, one of whom he recognized as the kidnapper of the lady he sought. And then he saw that she too stood by the pavilion. Pellinor spurred his horse forward and pushed between the two knights, forcing their duel to pause. Pellinor announced that the lady must return with him to Camelot. One of the knights, Meliot of Logres, told Pellinor that the lady was

GUINEVERE

Guinevere was Arthur's first and only queen. In Geoffrey of Monmouth's *Historia Regum Britanniae* she is of Roman blood, raised by Cador of Cornwall. In later legend she is the daughter of King Leodegrance, and when she and Arthur marry, her father's wedding gift to the king is the Round Table. Although she loves Arthur, she has a secret love of Lancelot, which eventually leads to the downfall of the Order of the Round Table and Arthur's reign as Pendragon. Heartbroken by the ensuing civil war, Guinevere ends her days as a nun.

A colourful depiction of knights jousting with ladies watching on in the background. Arthurian jousts often resulted in the riders being unhorsed and fighting on foot with sword and shield until one combatant became exhausted and allowed his guard to drop. (Alamy)

his cousin and he fought to rescue her; the other, Hontzlake of Wentland, lied aloud that he had won her by force of arms at the court of Arthur. Pellinor drew himself up in his saddle and told both men that the lady must go with him.

As Pellinor spoke, Hontzlake drove his sword into Pellinor's horse, which fell dead. Pellinor responded by removing that knight's head with a single blow. Turning to Meliot, he realized that the lady's defender was badly wounded. The injured knight asked Pellinor to protect his cousin by returning her to Arthur's court, and this they did, leaving Meliot at an abbey so that his wounds could be dressed.

A colourful depiction of Arthurian knights in battle, from the 15th-century French *Livre de Messire Lancelot du Lac*. (Bridgeman)

Traveling back to Camelot, Pellinor and his companion passed the lady who sat cradling the dead knight in her arms. She too had died by now, of grief, and Pellinor continued his journey back to Camelot having succeeded in his quest.

When the three knights returned to Camelot, Arthur and his new queen Guinevere sat in judgment, listening to each knight's adventures. They decided that Gawain had acted in haste but not with evil intent; he was allowed to go unpunished, but swore to protect women from that time henceforth, wherever he travelled. Tor was praised for returning with the white hound, but chastised for the death of Abelleus, killed at the request of a vengeful lady. Pellinor should not have refused help to a lady in need … and as Arthur told him this, the king beckoned Merlin forward with a further announcement.

The all-knowing Merlin explained that the lady who died cradling the wounded knight was Pellinor's daughter. He had not recognized her, as for many years he had never returned home, instead hunting a magical creature known as the Questing Beast. His daughter had grown up as a stranger to him, but lived happily with her lover until Hontzlake of Wentland slew him. Merlin explained that Pellinor had at least avenged his daughter, even though he did not intervene to save her.

The first quest of the Round Table had ended with some success and some failure; the well-intentioned misdeeds of these three knights were retold to each new member of the Order of the Round Table from that day on, ensuring that Arthur's knights would act with honour and chivalry forever more.

(OPPOSITE)
Gawain and his brother Gaheris charge into combat against Ablamor of the Marsh, on the Quest of the White Hart. Sadly, the hart lies dead before them and dishonour lies ahead of them. Gawain and Gaheris wear variations of the Orkney coat of arms belonging to their father King Lot, as shown in *D'Armagnac Armoral*; in *Gawain and the Green Knight*, the hero's coat of arms is described differently, as a yellow pentangle on a red background.

* * *

The First Quest of the Round Table was popularized in Malory's *Le Morte Darthur,* introducing the core concepts of Arthurian knighthood in one succinct story. As the events take place at Arthur's wedding, this adventure is the first time that the Order of the Round Table gather to serve their king. The three questing knights misjudge the situations they are in as they enthusiastically strive to carry out their king's command. Arthur and Guinevere's judgment on the knights at the end of the quest lays down some of the key values of chivalry: many Arthurian stories were as educational as they were entertaining.

The actions of the story's other characters also carry messages about the correct behaviour expected of a knight: the knights who attack Gawain and Gaheris nobly agree to release the brothers at the request of a lady; the same four knights are appalled by Gawain's bloody behaviour (a timely reminder of knighthood's moral code); and Felot and Petipace do as they are commanded by Tor, travelling unguarded to serve Arthur (as does Ablamor of the Marsh under Gawain's instruction).

King Pellinor (also known as Pellinore) was the King of the Isles, possibly alluding to the Scottish western isles or Anglesey off the coast of north Wales. He was most famous for his ceaseless but fruitless hunt of the Questing Beast (a strange creature with the head and neck of a snake, the body of a leopard, the rear of a lion, and the feet of a hart… and a noise emitted from its belly that sounded like 30 pairs of hunting dogs), although later versions of the tale replace him with the Saracen knight Palamedes. However, Pellinor should equally be remembered as the duelling knight who broke Arthur's Sword in the Stone when they first met… ultimately leading the king to seek a replacement in the form of Excalibur. After first being cast into a deep sleep by Merlin to end the duel, Pellinor served Arthur faithfully. Pellinor is a major character in the post-Vulgate Cycle and in Malory's reworking of those stories. In the musical *Camelot*, 'Pelly' is a comical character, who shows disdain for Arthur's idealistic approach to kingship.

In his earliest appearances, Tor is named as the son of a shepherd or cowherd; the post-Vulgate Cycle and Malory explain that he was the natural son of Pellinor, who forced himself onto Tor's mother before she later married a cowherd. Tor's royal lineage is revealed by Merlin when the boy arrives at Camelot. Towards the end of Arthur's reign, Guinevere is ordered to burn at the stake for her affair with Lancelot: Tor and his brother Aglovale are killed when Lancelot rides to her rescue.

Balin: The Knight with Two Swords

As she spoke, she dropped her cloak to the floor, revealing a well-crafted sword hanging from her waist in a scabbard. The task of the good knight she sought was to remove the sword from this scabbard. She had been cursed to wear it by the Lady of the Lake, the same faerie enchantress who had gifted another sword – the fabled blade Excalibur – to Arthur when he was crowned Pendragon. Ethereal and above all mysterious, not even the great wizard Merlin always understood the motives behind the Lady of the Lake's actions, including the curse bestowed upon Arthur's latest visitor.

As she stood displaying the scabbarded sword, the lady explained that this blade had brought her great misery; the removal of the sword from the scabbard by a worthy knight would end the enchantment and set her free.

Arthur moved forward to clasp the sword. First pulling gently and then with all his strength, he was unable to remove it from the scabbard. Pulling at his hardest, he managed to lift the lady from her feet and she begged him not to try so hard. Arthur stepped back and gestured to his knights; one at a time, led by Arthur's strong-arm nephew Gawain and Arthur's stepbrother Kay, each of the knights attempted to remove the sword. Each failed and the lady became ever more distressed.

Watching from the side of the hall was Balin. This young knight from the North did not lack bravery and nor did he lack the confidence to step forward, but he was newly released from captivity and out of favour in court. His crime had been to slay a cousin of Arthur, a miserable event indicative of the bad luck and hot head that accompanied Balin throughout his service as a knight. He watched with interest as each of Arthur's great knights tried and failed to remove the sword, and finally looking around the hall, he realized that he was the only one who had not yet tried. Thinking that his luck might

'The damsel warns Sir Balin.' Despite several chances to change the course of his adventure, Balin was fated to stumble continually into further woe. By HJ Ford.

The Lady of the Lake

The Lady of the Lake (also known as: Argante; Vivien; Nimue; Nineve) is best known as the kindly enchantress who gave Arthur the sword Excalibur, and as the magical underwater ruler who raised Lancelot and trained him as a skilled swordsman. Chrétien de Troyes explained that Lancelot was raised by a faerie queen and Ulrich von Zatzikhoven described her as living as a mermaid in an enchanted realm under the sea.

Elsewhere in Arthurian legend, she is a powerful enchantress who seals Merlin into a cave (or a tree, tomb, or tower), removing Arthur's most valued advisor from his court. Despite this, she also assists Arthur by saving him from a knight named Accolon (whom Morgan le Fay has presented with Excalibur in order to kill the king) and at another time by preventing him from putting on a cloak that would kill him (in another dastardly plot by Morgan). In the story of Balin she is killed when trying to reclaim her sword, although she is later one of the Ladies of Avalon who ferries the mortally wounded Arthur away to be healed after his final battle at Camlann. Tennyson removes her ambiguity and uses her as the epitome of evil, comparing her to a serpent.

These conflicting accounts and the variety of names for this sorceress cause confusion. The reality seems to be that there is more than one Lady of the Lake; it appears that 'Lady of the Lake' is a title for the faerie queen, whose identity changes during Arthur's reign and in stories by different authors.

change if he could prove his worth to Arthur, Balin asked to try the sword's hilt in an effort to show that he was a passingly good knight.

Both Arthur and the lady nodded their agreement, and to everyone's surprise – Balin's most of all – the sword glided easily out of the scabbard and the triumphant young knight held it aloft for all to see.

The lady smiled and brightened, but her delight was short lived as Balin refused to return the sword to her. Enchanted by its beauty and the unimaginable quality of the gleaming blade, Balin's chivalry deserted him. The lady broke into tears and fled the Great Hall with a parting warning that the blade would bring sorrow to any who used it.

Arthur turned to Balin to command him to return the sword, but before he spoke a chill descended on the hall and, preceded by a rolling low mist, the Lady of the Lady rode in on a shimmering white horse and floated gracefully from her mount to stand before Balin. Sometimes she acted for good, and sometimes for ill, but the sorceress was always welcomed at Camelot as Arthur's patron and sword-giver. Her celestial voice demanded the head of the knight who stood before her holding a sword that had been stolen from her. Her hand threw arcane gestures in the direction of Balin.

Balin's temper flared and he charged toward the faerie enchantress. Before anyone present in the Great Hall could stop him, he swung the sword in a power-charged arc and severed her head from her body. Crumpling to the floor as her mist dissipated from the hall, the Lady of the Lake instantaneously died in a lake of her own blood and Balin fled Camelot in panic, carrying both his own sword and the cursed sword stolen from the Lady of the Lake. Balin was now the Knight with Two Swords.

The court of Camelot was in shock and as Arthur stood in stunned silence over the Lady of the Lake's body, an Irish knight named Launceor rode out from the castle's gates. He was incensed at Balin's actions and the dishonour he had bestowed upon Arthur's court.

In a short time, he caught up with Balin and cried out a challenge. Balin turned his horse, and riding at full tilt towards his challenger, cut Launceor from his horse with the cursed sword. As so often happened Balin's temper rose, and he dismounted and strode towards his prone, dying enemy. At that very moment, a noble lady rode up and shouted that Balin had killed two hearts with his cursed blow.

As she said this, she drew a dagger and swung it at Balin shouting that Launceor was her lover. She had followed behind the Irish knight from Camelot and had witnessed his final duel. Calmer than before, Balin disarmed her and threw her to the ground to subdue her. As he turned back to Launceor, he heard a cry and spun round just in time to see the lady throw herself onto Balin's other sword. The lady died at the same moment as Launceor's wound gave way to death. Surrounded by death, Balin felt remorse.

Balin headed away from Camelot, living as an outcast and questing to redeem the wrongs he had caused. His heart full of regret, for he was not a wicked knight when calm, he headed north thinking that he might return to his homeland, and by chance met his brother Balan on the road. Balan listened to the ill fate that his brother had caused, and suggested that they ride together to defeat one of Arthur's greatest enemies: King Ryons of Wales. By doing so they hoped that Arthur would grant Balin forgiveness.

The brothers were formidable in battle, and the three swords of these two knights defeated King Ryons and 60 of his knights. With Balin's sword at his throat, Ryons swore allegiance to Arthur and surrendered himself at Camelot naming Balin as his conqueror. Some time later, as Arthur battled against the rebellious King Lot at Castle Tarabil, Balin and Balan fought beside their king and saved his life during the ferocious melee. Arthur accepted Balin back to Camelot, but remained wary of such an ill-fated knight. Having aided his brother's return to Arthur's court, Balan bade him farewell and the two knights went their separate ways.

Balin was determined to further redeem himself to Arthur, and travelled across Logres seeking misdeeds to set right. In all battles he was victorious, and he dissuaded a knight named Garnish of the Mount from killing himself after the desolate knight had beheaded the woman he loved in a jealous fury. Far from Camelot his path took him to a roadside cross, upon which was engraved: 'No knight alone must ride toward this castle.'

A maiden appeared on the track and advised Balin to turn back, but as she did so a horn blew in the distance: the signal of a knight's challenge. Balin would not refuse this. Following the path, Balin arrived at a small castle standing beside a river, and from its gates emerged the lady of the castle. Balin was welcomed into the castle and joined his hostess and a company of knights and ladies at a feast. When the feast ended the lady of the castle announced that he must now joust against a knight who waited on an island in the river, for no knight could feast at her castle without challenging him.

Balin agreed. His horse was weary but his heart was strong, and a worthy knight could not decline this customary joust. Looking at his armour, battered from so many hard-fought adventures, a knight at the feast took pity on him and offered him a fresh shield. With this new coat of arms, he rode down to the river and crossed to the island where the knight lived.

The huge horn that he had heard earlier in the day hung from a tree, and nearby sat a knight on horseback, armoured entirely in red. When this red knight saw that his challenger carried two swords he wondered if this could be the famous Balin, but the newcomer's shield told him otherwise. The knights saluted each other and put their horses into a canter as they lowered their lances. Each lance found the other knight's shield and both warriors were hurled from their saddles. The impact of the clash left them both stunned on the ground for several heartbeats, but both rose with sword in hand and set about each other. They were well matched, breaking each other's shields, hammering helmets tight onto skulls, and hacking through mail armour to draw blood. As he fought, Balin's temper began to rise and each new blow was delivered with increased vigour. As afternoon turned to sunset each knight had delivered seven terrible great wounds upon one another, but Balin gained the upper hand and delivered a winning blow with the Lady of the Lake's sword when his opponent's strength faltered.

Balin and the Holy Grail

Balin's story in *Le Morte Darthur* introduces the Holy Grail into the story of the Round Table. After his encounter with Launceor, Balin hears of a knight named Garlon who can make himself invisible: a power he uses dishonourably to slay other knights. Balin seeks out Garlon to avenge the murdered knights.

Garlon is the brother of King Pellam, and when Balin arrives at Pellam's castle he is asked to surrender his arms; being in possession of two swords he secretes the Lady of the Lake's sword under his cloak and hands over the other one. At a feast, Balin and Garlon argue and Balin draws his sword without warning – thus preventing Garlon from becoming invisible – and kills him.

Pellam chases Balin to avenge Garlon. Balin runs into a chapel where he finds a spear floating above a cup that sits upon an altar. In his rage, he takes the spear and pierces Pellam's side, even though the king has lowered his weapon and dropped to his knees upon seeing the cup in the chapel. Balin falls unconscious and is awoken by Merlin three days later in the now ruined castle.

Merlin explains to Balin that the cup is the Holy Grail and the spear is that used to wound Jesus on the cross: the Spear of Destiny. Pellam (also known as the Fisher King) is the guardian of the Grail and will live on in agony from the Dolorous Stroke delivered by Balin, until eventually healed by Galahad at the end of his Grail Quest. Galahad is also the eventual bearer of Balin's sword.

With this addition to Balin's tale, his role in the fate of Arthur and the Order of the Round Table becomes far more significant.

The Knight of the Island collapsed to the ground, bloodied, beaten, and dying. Balin was weak from his wounds and the length of the duel; he slumped beside his foe asking his name, for no knight before had ever been his match in battle.

The Red Knight forced his battered helmet from his head and announced that he was Balan, brother of Balin. And Balin forced off his own helmet to show his brother who had delivered the fatal blow. As he lay dying, Balan explained that he had been held captive and forced to fight ever since he killed the knight who had previously guarded the island. Both knights wept, and in each other's arms they died.

The lady of the castle buried the tragic brothers together in a tomb; not knowing Balin's name, she had inscribed only the name of Balan. But Merlin arrived at the tomb and added Balin's name. He took the Lady of the Lake's sword and embedded it into a magical stone, which floated down the river to Camelot where it would eventually present itself to the worthy knight Galahad.

Balin's good deeds earned his redemption at Camelot, yet he did not live to realize it.

'The death of Balin and Balan.' By HJ Ford.

* * *

The story of the ill-omened knight Balin (also known as Balyn; Balin Le Savage) was first told in *Suite du Merlin*, part of the post-Vulgate Cycle written in the 13th century. This was embellished in Malory's *Le Morte Darthur* in the 15th century, and substantially revised by Alfred Lord Tennyson in his 19th-century poem 'Balin the Savage'.

By drawing the Lady of the Lake's sword he proves that he is a 'passing good man', but despite this his impetuous actions and bad luck rarely desert him, and the fate of his brother is decided when Balin keeps the sword. The story warns that a knight should not show flair only in battle: he should take measured action and seek to put right any problems he is the cause of.

Perhaps uniquely of the famous knights who served Arthur, Balin was not a Knight of the Round Table: in most Arthurian chronologies, his story takes place before Arthur's wedding and therefore before the Order of the Round Table had been formed.

LANCELOT: THE KNIGHT OF THE CART

As was often the case, Arthur's stepbrother Kay had acted rashly. And as was often the case, his actions had put others in danger. This time Kay had rushed to accept the challenge of Meleagant, a tenacious knight who refused to serve Arthur, and a knight who would very clearly best Kay in a duel. Kay – known for his cruel wordplay more than his swordplay – had accepted before any of Arthur's better warriors could speak.

Meleagant had ridden fully armoured into Camelot just a moment before, his war-horse entering the Great Hall and stamping in circles as the mounted knight shouted challenges at Arthur and his knights. His sword drawn, he defied any warrior of Camelot to beat him in single combat. If this knight succeeded, he laughed, Meleagant would release the many good knights and ladies he held captive. But to fight him, Arthur's champion must ride into the forest beyond Camelot with Guinevere beside him.

Arthur could not dishonour Kay by replacing him so watched anxiously as Kay, Meleagant, and a subdued Guinevere rode from Camelot's gate. Gawain whispered in Arthur's ear that they should don their armour and follow, ready to rescue Guinevere when Kay was inevitably defeated. Arthur agreed.

'The Lady Nymue beareth away Launcelot into the Lake.' By Howard Pyle. The raising of Lancelot by the Lady of the Lake was an early addition to the story of Lancelot, sometimes rendering him Lancelot du Lac.

As Arthur, Gawain, and a handful of his most skilled warriors entered the forest, Kay's riderless horse flew past them. Spurring their own steeds forward, the knights realized that Kay had succumbed even faster than they had imagined, and that Meleagant had ridden away with Guinevere and the battered Kay, intending to add both to his growing dungeon of captives.

Giving chase through the forest, the riders came to a halt in front of an unknown knight standing beside an exhausted horse. This knight was Lancelot, unrecognized by them all, and he begged Gawain for a horse so that he could continue the pursuit of Meleagant; he had seen the capitulation of Kay and the kidnap of Guinevere and insisted that he should rescue her. On his fresh horse, Lancelot quickly outpaced the others and disappeared into the trees ahead of them.

As the chase continued Gawain also pulled ahead of Arthur's group, and along the forest trail he came across the horse he had given to Lancelot, ridden to an urgent death. A little further along the trail, he saw a dwarf driving a cart; alongside the cart stood Lancelot, asking the little man if he had seen Guinevere pass by. As Gawain rode closer, he heard the dwarf tell Lancelot that if he rode in the cart, he would discover the queen's whereabouts. Hesitating for a heartbeat, because only criminals were transported by cart, Lancelot hopped in. The dwarf asked Gawain if he too would ride in the cart, but Gawain was too proud to do so and remained on his horse.

Lancelot ignores the chivalric code by riding in a cart to rescue Guinevere, from *Romance of Lancelot of the Lake*, 1344. Gawain rides behind the cart. (Alamy)

Leaving the forest the cart trundled through villages and farmland, and the local folk mocked the shameful knight in the cart and threw rotting turnips and dung at him. Lancelot did not care, such was his desire to free Guinevere, but the courtly Gawain rode at a distance.

Arriving at a crossroads the dwarf halted the cart as Lancelot busied himself brushing off animal dung and vegetable matter. The dwarf gestured for him to get out. A lady stood at the crossroads with a fresh horse, as if waiting for Lancelot, and both knights approached her. She explained that she knew of Guinevere's fate: the queen had been taken by Meleagant to his realm, which could only be entered with great tribulation. From this land no foreigner had ever returned, and it could be entered in only one of two ways: slowly via an underwater bridge that wound across a river at waist depth, or more swiftly by the sword bridge, a razor-sharp blade that spanned a chasm. Mounting the fresh horse, Lancelot headed for the Sword Bridge and Gawain quested for the underwater bridge. Although he did not know it at the time, Gawain's route slowed his pursuit so much that only Lancelot stood a chance of freeing Guinevere.

Approaching a stream, Lancelot's path was blocked by a knight who three times warned him not to cross. Ignoring this warning in his hasty pursuit, Lancelot rushed on but was knocked from his steed by the knight's sword. Pulling the knight from his horse, Lancelot crushed his opponent's legs between his strong arms until he agreed to a fair fight when Lancelot was ready. Quickly agreeing, both knights jousted and Lancelot felled the Knight of the Ford with a single blow, riding on with all speed.

Across the stream, Lancelot rode through meadowland and rolling hills. Still he followed the path of Meleagant, and on a flat rock beside a spring he noticed something glinting in the afternoon sun. It was a golden comb entwined with golden hair. This he recognized as Guinevere's comb, and the very thought of her made him swoon. Recovering himself, Lancelot placed the comb inside his surcoat, close by his heart. He raced on.

'How Sir Launcelot rode errant in a cart.' By Howard Pyle.

Lancelot's next encounter was with a proud knight who mocked him for thinking that he might cross the sword bridge, and even more so for having ridden in a prisoners' cart. Tempers rose and the two knights duelled, killing each other's horses at the first impact of the joust. Lancelot rose with deft speed and battered the mocking knight into submission, stopping when his stricken foe begged for mercy. As he did so, a lady in dishevelled robes rode up on a mule and demanded that Lancelot present her with the knight's head: despite his proud demeanour she claimed him to be a base and faithless knight and insisted that to kill him would be a good and charitable act. Unsure whether to grant the lady her request or offer the knight the mercy he begged for, Lancelot decided that they should fight on and see what happened. But, he announced, he would make it easier for his opponent by standing on the spot as they fought, not moving but relying on his swordsmanship alone. Such was Lancelot's skill with a sword that he easily fended off the knight's furious assault, and with one great hack the mocking knight's head fell from his shoulders. The lady's request granted, Lancelot rushed on once more.

And so he came to the sword bridge. The chasm below was deep and at the bottom of a sheer drop swirled a foaming black, roaring river. The bridge itself was the finest and sharpest tightrope of a blade he had ever touched, and each end was wedged into a tree stump.

Galahad

Galahad was the son of Lancelot. He was the perfect knight, and in the Vulgate Cycle and Malory's *Le Morte Darthur*, he completes the Quest of the Holy Grail before being spirited away to become the Grail's new guardian.

At the Round Table, Galahad is the only knight able to sit at the Siege Perilous, a seat magically reserved for the purest of men. The sword stolen from the Lady of the Lake by Balin, which Merlin embedded in a stone and floated to Camelot, can only be drawn by Galahad and becomes his own sword. Not only is Galahad a pure knight, but he is also a capable fighter: when he first arrives at Camelot, he bests all of the knights in a tournament except his father Lancelot, Gawain, Bors, and Perceval.

Soon after Galahad's entrance to the Order of the Round Table, the Grail appeared, limiting the extent of stories about his non-Grail adventures. Galahad was a relatively late addition to Arthurian legend, possibly introduced to allow a more pious knight to complete the Grail Quest than had previously been the case.

Lancelot crosses the Sword Bridge on his hands and knees, and then proceeds to rescue the queen from a tower (guarded here by lions) in this mid-14th-century manuscript. (Alamy)

Lancelot removed the mailed armour from his feet and hands to gain better purchase and ran onto the sword. The sharp metal sliced into his feet and he momentarily swayed over the chasm, seeming as if he would fall. Dropping to crawl along, Lancelot sped along the sword, the blade cutting ever deeper into his hands and feet. If he slowed, the wounds would be less severe … but if he slowed, he would take longer to reach Guinevere.

Reaching the far side of the chasm, Lancelot rolled off the bridge in agony and sat for just a moment to bind his wounds. As he did so, he noticed for the first time a great tower standing in the distance. This, he knew, would be where Meleagant had taken the queen.

Journeying as swiftly as he could on his bleeding feet, Lancelot dragged himself to the castle where that great tower stood. News that a gallant knight had braved the sword bridge had travelled quickly, and a great throng of people had gathered in the castle's courtyard to watch what would happen next. Some of the crowd wore hair shirts and went barefoot in an attempt to bring divine intervention to the aid of this new knight; others who supported Meleagant prayed for his victory.

Passing through the castle gate into the busy courtyard, Lancelot saw Meleagant standing fully armed and armoured, taking practice swings with his sword. He was playing to the crowd, and did so even more as he gestured to his guards to bring Guinevere out. The captive queen's hands were bound, and as she stood surrounded by Meleagant's guardsmen, Lancelot drew his sword and advanced on her kidnapper.

Sword clattered onto shield, and the duellists rained increasingly heavy blows onto one another. Lancelot, weakened by the wounds from the sword bridge, mustered all of his strength to fend off Meleagant's hacking blade and sheltered behind his shield. As he did so, he realized that he could not take his eyes from Guinevere. Her beauty was such to him that even in this life or death fray, he could think only of her and had to gaze in wonder at her charm. A heavy blow on his shield refocused him on Meleagant.

Lancelot was a tremendous fighter, but Meleagant was hardly weaker; it

KAY

Kay (also known as Cai) features in many tales of the Round Table, often sly or arrogant at the beginning of an adventure and humbled by better knights before the adventure ends. He was Arthur's foster brother, and both boys were raised by Kay's father Ector at the request of Merlin; when Arthur was appointed Pendragon of Logres he bestowed upon Kay the honour of being Camelot's steward. Kay's behaviour, so often belligerent and cynical, can be interpreted as a warning to real-life knights about how they should *not* act: chivalry and humility always won through against Kay's behaviour. Despite his discourtesy, Kay was always a loyal servant to Arthur and eventually died in the war against Mordred. In Welsh legend, Cai was a regular companion of the warlord Arthur (along with a warrior named Bedwyr, who featured in later legend as the knight Bedivere).

was no wonder that Kay had been defeated with such ease or that the castle's dungeon was full of brave knight prisoners from the Order of the Round Table. Gradually the rebellious knight gained the advantage over his weakened and distracted opponent. Lancelot found himself forced back under a hail of blows so that Guinevere was behind him and no longer in his sight. Desperate to look at her once again, Lancelot turned his head, no longer focusing on winning the battle and doing no more than deflecting Meleagant's sword cuts with his own sword held behind his back. The crowd loved this skilful display, but victory was slipping from him: on his knees and desperately parrying attacks, he still looked away from his enemy to gaze instead at the beautiful queen.

'Sir Launcelot of the Lake.' By Howard Pyle.

From a window high in the castle, a kindly lady noticed why Lancelot was distracted. Above the noise of the crowd, he heard her voice call out to him. She told him to fight his way around Meleagant and attack from the other side, so that he could face his opponent and still gaze at the queen. Inspired by this notion, Lancelot rose from the ground and deftly danced around Meleagant's heavy blows. Now facing Meleagant with the queen in view over her kidnapper's shoulder, Lancelot unleashed a series of vicious sword cuts onto his enemy, ignoring his own wounds by thinking only of freeing Guinevere.

Meleagant, powerful though he was, fell to the ground and offered his sword to Lancelot. Defeated but not willing to die, he yielded the fray and was carried away to have his wounds tended by his followers. Lancelot stood with Guinevere for a moment, before she walked away without meeting his eyes.

Lancelot was distraught but carried on with his knightly duty, freeing the prisoners from the dungeon. Kay sheepishly emerged along with many other knights and ladies; he had been well beaten by Meleagant and bore the wounds to prove it. Lancelot doubted that this would subdue his quick tongue for more than a few days.

As the procession of freed knights and ladies journeyed back to Camelot, meeting the soggy Gawain on the way, Lancelot pondered why Guinevere had so snubbed him. It was – of course – the gallant knight's hesitation at climbing into the cart so early in the chase: his fear of the shame that this would bring to him, albeit for no more than a heartbeat's thought, had momentarily outweighed his devotion to saving his queen. Guinevere did eventually forgive Lancelot, but from that day on he never paused to place his own pride before her safety.

* * *

Lancelot (also known as: Launcelot; Lancelot of the Lake; Launcelot du Lac; Lanzelet; Lancilotto) is without doubt the best known of the Knights of the Round Table. He is consistently portrayed as a stunning warrior and a handsome fellow: many knights fall to his sword and many ladies seek his attention.

Lancelot arrived at the court of Camelot led by the Lady of the Lake; orphaned from the royal family of King Ban of Benwick (Burgundy in modern day France) as a boy, the faerie queen had raised him in her underwater realm and schooled him in battle and chivalry. A skilled swordsman and jouster, he was to become Arthur's champion and Guinevere's lover, in part responsible for the downfall of Logres' greatest king.

Chrétien de Troyes introduced the character of Lancelot to Arthurian legend in *Le Chevalier de la Charrette*, the story told in this chapter; whether Chrétien invented him or whether Lancelot existed as an obscure character before this is not known, but many later versions of Arthurian legend use this quest to introduce Lancelot to the court of Camelot, only naming him part way through the story. Chrétien's story takes place over a number of days and includes many further challenges for Lancelot, although I abridge the plot into a shorter chase. Lancelot's love for Guinevere is present even in this early tale of his deeds: not only does he single-mindedly pursue her kidnapper, but at a later point in the story, she attempts to commit suicide when she believes him to be dead, and Lancelot attempts suicide when he believes she is dead.

Lancelot's character is more fully developed in the Vulgate and post-Vulgate Cycle, which evolved Chrétien's work to include tales of Lancelot's childhood, his early adventures, and his quest for the Holy Grail.

After Lancelot's affair with Guinevere was exposed to Arthur, the king prepared to burn his queen at the stake. Lancelot rescued her, splitting the allegiance of the Order of the Round Table and killing several leading knights in the process. After Arthur's death, Lancelot became a monk and died six weeks after Guinevere.

(OVERLEAF)
Lancelot battles Meleagant to rescue Guinevere. His hands and feet have been cut open by the Sword Bridge that he crossed to reach the queen as quickly as he could. Lancelot is enamoured with the queen and turns to gaze at her throughout the fight; from a high window a kindly lady advises Lancelot to manoeuvre around his opponent so that he can face forward and still see the queen. The coat of arms worn by Lancelot in this plate is based on that shown in a French manuscript *c.* 1300; Meleagant's is based on *D'Armagnac Armoral*.

Lancelot and the Four Queens

It was a scorching summer's day, and Lancelot had ridden out with his nephew Lionel, looking for adventure. Shading themselves under an ancient tree as they rested their horses, Lancelot's eyes slowly closed and he slept peacefully. Lionel remained alert, and after some time had passed, three riders came into view. As they drew closer, Lionel saw that they were knights galloping in a fearful panic. Behind them came a fourth knight, a warrior with great horns on his helmet, and he overtook the other horsemen in turn, smiting each from their saddle with a powerful blow from his axe. Dismounting, the horned knight bound his three prisoners and started to lead them away slung over their own saddles.

Lionel mounted his horse and gave pursuit, not stopping to wake Lancelot. He overtook the horned knight and challenged him. Turning to receive Lionel's charge, the horned knight dealt him such a heavy blow that both rider and horse collapsed to the ground. When he came to, Lionel realized that he too was bound and hanging over his saddle, led away to the castle of the horned knight. Once there, each of the prisoners was stripped and flayed with thorns, and then thrown into a dark dungeon alongside many other knights who had fallen victim to the horned knight.

Lionel's brother Ector de Maris had set out after Lancelot and Lionel, hoping to join them on a quest. He met not with the sleeping Lancelot, but

The Vulgate Cycle

In the early 13th century a group of French Cistercian monks wrote a series of Arthurian adventures based on the earlier works of Geoffrey of Monmouth, Wace, and Robert de Boron, but focusing on the romance of Lancelot and Guinevere and the quest for the Holy Grail. These five tales were: *Lancelot du Lac*, *Queste del Saint Graal*, *Estoire del Saint Graal*, *Mort Artu*, and *Estoire de Merlin.* Collectively they are known as the Vulgate Cycle (and sometimes as the *Prose Lancelot*).

These five stories greatly influenced later Arthurian legend, including a series of works known as the post-Vulgate Cycle, which added to or reworked the detail of some of the tales. The Vulgate and post-Vulgate Cycles introduced Arthurian love affairs, morality, and stronger religious elements than had previously been present in Arthurian legend, demonstrating these qualities through the actions of the knight heroes.

instead with a forester, whom he asked where adventure could be found. The forester explained that he should keep riding until he found a tree upon which hung the many-colored shields of the good knights defeated by Turquin the horned knight. At the tree, Ector should beat on the copper drum hanging there and prepare himself for defeat. Ector thanked him and rode on, also destined to be beaten and thrown naked into Turquin's dungeon.

Lancelot, meanwhile, dreamt many a joyous dream. His sleep was not disturbed by the arrival of four queens of great beauty. With the four queens rode four knights, holding a canopy to shade the ladies from the summer heat. As they passed Lancelot, the queens stopped to admire the handsome young knight. As they watched him sleep, they began to argue over which of them could make this sleeping knight into their lover. One of the four, Morgan Le Fay – Arthur's sister and enemy – was an enchantress of great repute, and cast a spell on Lancelot to make him sleep for another quarter of a day. She explained that she would take him to her castle, remove the enchantment of sleep and replace it with a binding of iron chains, and then make him choose one of the queens as his paramour. One of them, she said, would eventually have him.

'How four queens found Launcelot sleeping.' By Aubrey Beardsley; Beardsley's first commission as an artist was to illustrate JM Dent & Co's 1893 *Le Morte d'Arthur*.

The bespelled Lancelot was carried away by the queens' knights and placed under lock and key. When he awoke from the spell, Morgan Le Fay introduced the other queens: the Queens of Northgales, Eastland, and the Outer Isles. She then instructed him to choose his lover. Although he thought each of them was beautiful, he could not choose between them, for he loved another. Lancelot explained that he would not, and should rather remain imprisoned. And so he remained in the dungeon, answering the question in the same way every day. The queens grew frustrated but Lancelot still refused to play their game. His salvation came in the form of the serving girl who brought his food every day. She too was a captive, a daughter of Duke Rocedon who desperately needed a courageous champion to fight in a tournament against the King of Northgales the next day. In return for the keys to his cell, Lancelot promised to fight for her father. And with that, both captives fled the castle.

As the next day dawned, Lancelot prepared to fight as Rocedon's champion, and carried a plain white shield so that no-one would know his true identity. Fighting on behalf of the King of Northgales were three Knights of the Round Table – Mordred, Mador de la Porte, and Gahalantine – but Lancelot bested them all. Hacking away in the centre of the melee amidst the throng of scores of battered and battering knights, Lancelot delivered a blow to the King of Northgales that broke his thigh, and remained the only knight standing at the end of the day. Duke Rocedon's champion had prevailed.

Lancelot in Love

When the queens asked the captive Lancelot which of them he would love, he was unable to do so because he loved another. Morgan Le Fay, with her magical powers, knew who this was: Arthur's wife, Guinevere. In Malory's *Le Morte Darthur*, this plot device is announced early in the story and acts as a backdrop to many of Lancelot's later adventures. Lancelot and Guinevere's relationship is always kept discreet, although for a time Lancelot runs mad in the forest due to his love of the queen. Their liaisons are eventually revealed by Mordred, sparking a civil war between Arthur on one side and Lancelot on the other... events escalate and result at the end of Arthur's reign at the battle of Camlann.

Although Lancelot loved Guinevere this did not stop his involvement with other women, including two ladies named Elaine. Elaine of Astolat was Tennyson's famous Lady of Shalott, who fell in love with Lancelot from afar and when this remained unrequited, she committed suicide, floating down the river to Camelot in a barge. Elaine of Carbonek was rescued by Lancelot from both a scalding bath and a dragon; Elaine tricked Lancelot into thinking she was Guinevere, and after they slept together, Elaine gave birth to Lancelot's son Galahad. A third Elaine was important to Lancelot: his mother, the wife of King Ban of Benwick.

The love between Lancelot and Guinevere was present from Lancelot's earliest introduction to Arthurian legend, eventually leading to the downfall of Arthur's kingdom. By C Walter Hodges.

Thankful for Lancelot's help and the safe return of his daughter, Rocedon asked Lancelot his name. Upon discovering he was a Knight of the Round Table, the old man's face lit up as he realized how he could repay his champion: a false knight named Turquin held in his dungeon three score Knights of the Round Table. None had yet outfought him but, the grateful duke exclaimed, a warrior as fine as Lancelot stood a better chance than any other knight in Logres. Lancelot mounted his horse and rode to find Turquin.

As Lancelot approached the tree from which the shields of the fallen knights swung, a horse slowly approached. On the horse, Gawain's brother Gaheris lay slumped with a terrible wound, another victim of Turquin; Gaheris had fought valiantly yet in vain, and his horse had carried him clear of Turquin's intended humiliation. Lancelot struck the copper drum and awaited the horned knight.

Barely a birdsong later, as the drum still rang, Turquin appeared. The two knights spurred their horses at one another. Lances smashed on shields, and the collision held such force as to break both horses' backs. On foot the two combatants came eagerly together and laid about each other with sword and axe. Such was the strength and ferocity of the duel that shields shattered and broken armour fell to the floor. They fought for two hours, until both collapsed, exhausted.

Between heavy breaths, Lancelot asked why Turquin so hated the Round Table. Turquin explained that one of their number – Lancelot of the Lake – had slain his brother Carados, and in return Turquin had slain a hundred of Arthur's knights and maimed as many again. Still carrying the white shield from the tournament, Lancelot was unknown to Turquin, but revealed his true identity as the duel resumed. Each knight went at the other like a wild bull, fighting for two hours more before Lancelot wrestled his opponent to the floor, tore off his helmet, and cut his head from his body.

'Sir Launcelot doeth battle with Sir Turquine.' By Howard Pyle.

From the castle of the defeated Turquin, Lancelot released Lionel, Ector de Maris, and many other sorely wounded knights. Having rested and recovered his strength, Lancelot defeated yet more dishonourable knights and a pair of giants who terrorized the land. Returning to Camelot, he recounted his deeds, and from that time on Lancelot was renowned as the greatest knight in the world, and most honoured by the Order of the Round Table as Arthur's new champion.

* * *

This story first appeared in the French prose *Lancelot Propre* (written in the early 13th century), although in this original version only three queens hold the knight prisoner. By the time of Malory, a fourth queen was added and the lord whom Lancelot championed had changed from Rocedon to Bagdemagus, the father of Meleagant in *The Knight of the Cart*.

As usual, Morgan appears as an enemy of Arthur's despite their blood relation, and her demand of Lancelot to choose a lover forces him to demonstrate that his true love is Guinevere: a fact not lost on the enemies of Arthur.

The tale is not without medieval humour; after his escape from Morgan Le Fay, Lancelot rests for the night in an empty pavilion and is awakened by a bearded face kissing him. Jumping out of the bed, Lancelot discovers that the knight who owns the pavilion has returned, believing that the warm sleeper in his bed is his wife.

(OVERLEAF)
As Lancelot sleeps under a tree, Morgan Le Fay and the Queens of Northgales, Eastland, and the Outer Isles ride up. Intrigued by his good looks, the four queens have decided to carry him away and hold him as their prisoner until he chooses one of them as his lover. The coat of arms shown for the sleeping Lancelot is one of the most commonly worn designs for him in medieval manuscripts from the 13th century onwards.

GAWAIN AND THE GREEN KNIGHT

On the first day of a new year the snow fell deep around Camelot. As was his custom, Arthur held a feast to celebrate the coming year and his followers gathered in the warmth of the Great Hall. Scarcely had the guests taken their seats when a howling wind flung open the heavy wooden doors and in a flurry of snow a giant of a knight rode in, a vision of green.

His green skin was clad in green armour, around which was wound holly. His bushy great beard was green, as was his hair, and from both sprouted yet more flora. His horse was equally green and bedecked with green leaves. In his hand he gripped a sharp-bladed battle-axe, and his eyes shone red as he rumbled out a deep-voiced challenge to any brave knight present.

The headless Green Knight in Arthur's hall, from the *Gawain and the Green Knight* manuscript, *c.* 1375–1400. (Bridgeman)

Gawain leapt forward ahead of any other knight, and accepted on behalf of his uncle the king. The Green Knight had not yet explained the nature of the challenge, but did so now. Each of them would strike one blow against the other and the better man would be the winner. He threw his giant axe to Gawain's feet, and Arthur's brave nephew hefted it. He would strike first.

The Green Knight dismounted, and strode across the hall to kneel before Gawain, exposing his neck and asking Gawain to deliver a blow when he was ready to do so. Gawain brought the axe down heavily and cleanly onto the giant's neck. The sharp blades sliced through flesh and bone, and the Green Knight's head fell to the floor. No return blow would be struck, Gawain thought to himself.

But then the outcry began. The Green Knight's body began to stand, even though his green bearded head lay some distance across the paved floor. Unsteady at first, but then standing firm, the green torso moved across the hall to recover its detached head and lifted it aloft. The unseeing eyes flashed red once more, and spoke out loud that one year to the day, they must meet at the Green Chapel where Gawain would receive his blow in return.

The Green Knight tucked his head under his arm, remounted his green horse, and slowly departed the hall. As the doors closed out the snow and the feast resumed, the court of Camelot had little appetite.

Least of all Gawain.

The year passed quickly for Gawain; as summer ended he set out from Camelot to find the mysterious Green Chapel, heading north for want of better direction. As Gawain rode and enquired about the chapel without success, winter set in. The further north he travelled, the more the snow settled on the uplands and the woodland trees lost their leaves. Gawain ploughed forward through icicled forests and crossed frozen rivers. His armour sat cold against his flesh. Still none could give him directions to the Green Chapel.

Only three nights from his appointment with the Green Knight, Gawain crested a snowy hill and saw before him a small castle sheltered in the valley below. Cold and in need of a meal, he headed towards it.

Sean Connery's monumental Green Knight prepares to remove the head of Gawain (played by Miles O'Keeffe) in 1984's *Sword of the Valiant*. (Alamy)

The lord of the castle met him at the gate and cordially welcomed him. Bercilak, as was the lord's name, explained that few visitors found his home and that a nephew of Arthur was doubly welcome to his hospitality. Changed into warm, dry garments Gawain was introduced to Bercilak's wife; Lady Bercilak was a vision of beauty tempered only by the wizened old crone who stood always by her side. The crone was her mother, whose cold dark eyes viewed Gawain with suspicion.

As darkness fell Gawain was summoned to a fine dinner, where he asked if Bercilak knew of the Green Chapel. The chapel, Bercilak explained, lay close by and he would set the questing knight on the correct path once he had rested with them for a few days. This suited Gawain and he relaxed into the feast, courteous as ever a knight should be to the lord and lady of a castle.

Before retiring to sleep, Bercilak explained that he would set off early in the morning snow to hunt for the next day's table; Gawain, he said, should rest, but they must agree to exchange whatever winnings came their way on the following day. An odd suggestion, Gawain thought, but bowed his acceptance and went to his warm bed.

As he awoke on a hazy, cold winter morning Gawain heard Bercilak and his huntsmen leaving the castle. A few moments later came a soft knock at his door and Lady Bercilak appeared. This time her mother was absent. She sat beside Gawain on the bed and jested with him in word games. Each amused

Bercilak's wife visits Gawain in his bedchamber, from the *Gawain and the Green Knight* manuscript, *c.* 1375–1400.

the other, even though the courteous Gawain spurned the lady's advances, and when the time came for Lady Bercilak to busy herself for her husband's return, she gifted Gawain a fine red-gold ring from her finger as a token of their friendship.

Bercilak clattered into the castle courtyard followed by his huntsmen staggering under the weight of a freshly slain boar. Calling to Gawain, Bercilak offered the boar as his winnings from the day and asked Gawain to share the results of his own toils. Gawain dutifully presented the ring he had been given but Bercilak refused to accept it: he cheerily said that the ring must have been given to Gawain as a token of a lady's love, and that he could not take that from Gawain. With that, he waved away the day's exchange and shared the boar with Gawain anyway.

Over dinner that night of wild boar, with both Lady Bercilak and her mother present, the lord of the castle made the same agreement with Gawain: each would share their winnings from the next day's toil. Lady Bercilak's mother glowered furiously at Gawain.

Once again, Gawain awoke to the sound of Bercilak's hunting party leaving in the early morning light; and once again a soft knock came at his door. The lady sat with Gawain just as she had the previous day, and each enjoyed the other's company even though the virtuous Gawain spurned her alluring advances. As she left, the lady kissed Gawain on the cheek and left his chamber. Shortly afterwards, Bercilak arrived with the warm carcass of a great stag and shared his winnings with Gawain. In return Gawain embraced his host and kissed him on the cheek. Bercilak chuckled to himself about this frivolous gift and went about the rest of his day a happy man. At dinner, as they ate the stag, the old crone stared daggers at Gawain but said nothing. Bercilak and Gawain agreed to continue their arrangement the next day, the visiting knight unwilling to disagree with his host.

As Gawain lay down that night, he realized that the next day was the start of a new year, and that in the morning he must face the Green Knight. Thinking of Lady Bercilak instead, he drifted into sleep. When he awoke, Gawain lay in bed pondering the day ahead: his honour meant that he must ride to the Green Chapel, even if it meant he would die. He would not let down the honour of the Round Table by failing to appear.

As Bercilak left the castle on his daily hunt, his wife once again appeared in Gawain's chamber. As before, they talked, played word games, and enjoyed their time together; as before, Gawain spurned Lady Bercilak's amorous intentions out of respect for his host. But as they talked, she explained that she knew a way for Gawain to guard himself against the Green Knight: she held out a green baldric edged with gold for him to wear around his waist. This, she said, would magically protect him from the Green Knight's blow. Gawain did not at first accept this gift, as magical protection would be dishonourable for a knight facing his plight; but then he thought of his time with Lady Bercilak and pondered that it would be a fine thing to survive his encounter at the Green Chapel and see her once more.

He accepted the baldric, and Lady Bercilak left him with a kiss on each cheek. When the lord of the castle returned from the hunt with a fox, in return Gawain kissed both his cheeks but did not surrender the baldric. Later in the morning, lord, lady, and the wizened crone watched Gawain leave for the Green Chapel. The lord and lady wished him luck; the old crone said nothing but looked content for the first time since Gawain arrived.

The hazy midwinter sun held no warmth as Gawain followed the path he had been told about. Deeper into the valley he rode, and deeper the snow became. Eventually, he dismounted and led his horse through the deepening whiteness. Approaching the chapel, he felt weak and he watched the Green Knight emerge to greet him. The green head was back atop the green body, and in his hand he held the same sharpened axe that Gawain had swung at Camelot one year past.

He gestured Gawain to kneel before him. Even though he wore the green baldric that Lady Bercilak promised would protect him, Gawain had to fight hard to prevent himself from turning and fleeing. But his knight's duty meant that he must accept the challenge or shame his king. He pretended to be fearless, afraid to show his dread.

Gawain knelt and the Green Knight swung the axe at his exposed neck. A hair's breadth from the flesh, the Green Knight stopped the blade, and Gawain flinched. The Green Knight mocked him, reminding the Knight of the Round Table that he himself had neither flinched nor fled a year before. Gawain responded that if his head fell from his shoulders, he could not stoop down to put it back on.

Regaining his courage, Gawain knelt once again. The Green Knight swung the axe a second time, and a second time he stopped a fraction from Gawain's neck. He mocked once again and Gawain shouted at him to strike a third time and be done with it. The blade fell through the air a third time and nicked the back of Gawain's neck, but left nothing more than a flesh wound. Gawain sprang up: he had survived the challenge and now intended to fell the Green Knight in a duel.

But before him stood Bercilak, not the Green Knight. Gawain lowered his sword and Bercilak explained that he had been a bespelled prisoner of Morgan le Fay, the foul sorceress sworn to oppose Arthur and his knights. Bercilak had been tricked by her and cursed to perform as the Green Knight, sent to

In the bleak midwinter Gawain approaches the Green Chapel, beckoned forth by the Green Knight. Gawain's heraldry in the poem is clearly described, differing from the usual coat of arms allocated to him. By Alan Lathwell.

Camelot to humiliate Arthur and his cowardly servants. She had not expected any knight to search for the Green Chapel after seeing the headless Green Knight stride from Camelot, but once Gawain set off, she resided at Bercilak's castle in the guise of his wife's mother. The curse now broken by Gawain's determination to serve his king regardless of his own death, she would by now have fled and Bercilak was no longer held in her power.

Gawain asked Bercilak why he had delivered three blows. Each had been given as a result of Gawain's deceit and disregard shown to his host: one swing for each morning Gawain had spent with Lady Bercilak. The final blow would not even have cut into Gawain's neck if he had been honest and offered the green baldric to Bercilak in exchange for the fox. But if Gawain had not refused Lady Bercilak's amorous advances, the end result would have been far bloodier.

When Gawain returned to Camelot, Arthur decreed that green baldrics were to be worn forever after by the Order of the Round Table, as a reminder of a knight's duty to be honourable and chivalrous.

* * *

Gawain (also known as: Gawaine; Gauvain; Walewein; Gwalchmai) was one of the greatest and most loyal Knights of the Round Table, serving Arthur faithfully from Arthur's wedding day to Gawain's death in the catastrophic civil war culminating with Arthur's fall.

Gawain was Arthur's nephew (a son of King Lot of Orkney and Arthur's half-sister Morgause) and acted as his champion before and after Lancelot; alongside Lancelot and Tristan, Gawain is the most prominent of Arthur's knights in medieval and modern literature. Gawain's character most usually defines love, valour, and courtesy – the ideal knight and a protector of women – but some stories cast him as a boorish or uncouth knight.

Gawain is a favourite hero of the brutal adventures so beloved of Middle English literature, and also features in Scottish, German, and Dutch tales. He dies fighting for Arthur against the treacherous Mordred in Geoffrey of Monmouth's work, and by Lancelot's sword in other versions including Malory's; shortly before his death, he writes a letter to Lancelot asking the errant hero to return to aid Arthur and forgiving him for slaying Gawain's brothers Gareth and Gaheris.

Gawain features in some early Welsh Arthurian traditions as a hero named Gwalchmai, who is the son of Arthur's sister and one of his leading warriors. It has been suggested that the origin of Gawain may have been as a pre-Christian sun god, as his strength is noted as growing towards noon and declining as the sun's strength weakens through the afternoon.

Gawain, incidentally, is mentioned in passing in the movie *Monty Python and the Holy Grail*, as one of the knights slain by the Killer Rabbit of Caerbannog's 'nasty, big, pointy teeth'!

The surviving manuscript of *Sir Gawain and the Green Knight* was written around 1370–90, probably in the British West Midlands. Gawain was a popular Arthurian character in Britain and featured in a number of stories from the British Isles in the 14th century. The language of the poem is rich and rewarding, heavy in medieval symbolism and period detail, and like many other Arthurian tales the work is an instructional piece on knightly virtue.

The story has been shown on film several times: *Gawain and the Green Knight* (1973), *Sword of the Valiant* (1983), and TV movie *Gawain and the Green Knight* (1991).

GAWAIN AND THE LOATHLY LADY

Deep in the wild forests far north of Camelot, Arthur had outpaced his hounds and fellow huntsmen. But as he stood over the carcass of his newly slain stag the silence of the forest was broken as a huge knight clad in black armour rode before him, crashing through the undergrowth to holler a battle cry. Caught off guard and equipped for hunting rather than battle, Arthur was at the black knight's mercy and was knocked to the ground.

Pinned down by the tip of the black knight's black lance, Arthur could do little but yield. Holding Arthur in place with the lance's sharp tip, the knight revealed himself to be Gromer Somer Joure. Gromer hated Arthur as the king had confiscated much of his land as a punishment and awarded it to Gawain. This giant of a knight gave Arthur two choices: to die now with a single lance thrust to his heart, or to answer a riddle.

Arthur chose the latter, and Gromer asked: 'What do women most desire?'

That was all. Gromer told Arthur to seek him out a year from this day and to answer correctly or forfeit his life. With that, he turned his horse around and cantered away.

Shaken but still alive, Arthur slowly rode back to his hunting lodge, his mind no longer on the stag he had killed. Upon his return, Gawain was the first to notice that all was not well and asked Arthur what had happened. With the day's strange event explained to him, Gawain immediately offered his services to Arthur and they agreed to travel far and wide across the kingdom to find an answer to Gromer's riddle.

For nearly a full year both Arthur and Gawain rode throughout the land,

'King Arthur findeth ye old woman in ye hut.' By Howard Pyle, demonstrating his masterful command of Ye Olde English.

MORDRED

Mordred, best known as Arthur's evil nephew, is actually revealed in most versions of Arthurian legend to be Arthur's son: his mother was Arthur's half-sister Morgause, who knowingly or accidentally seduces her brother to conceive Mordred. Mordred arrives at Camelot at the age of 14 and becomes a Knight of the Round Table. Carrying out his duty as one of Arthur's knights, Mordred and his brother Agravaine reveal the love affair between Guinevere and Lancelot, leading to civil war and Arthur's eventual downfall. Left in charge of Logres when Arthur's army marches on Lancelot, Mordred usurps his uncle, leading to the death of both at the battle of Camlann.

seeking audience with wise men, hermits, wizards, and the eldermen of every village they visited. Both kept a parchment listing the answers they were given, although few of the men they questioned had a likely answer. Downhearted, Arthur and Gawain returned to Camelot to compare notes.

A few days before the full year passed, Arthur prepared himself for the journey to meet Gromer and deliver his answer. He could not answer the riddle, but as an honourable knight he could not go back on his word. He rode to meet Gromer, accepting his fate.

Passing through the same forest as he had a year before, Arthur rode past an old hag, who called out to him. She called out, saying that she could tell him what women most desire. In return, she said as she absent-mindedly scratched her behind, Gawain must ask her to marry him.

Arthur turned in his saddle and looked at this hag. She wore foul tattered robes, squatted with the stature of a swollen toad, and the features of her face seemed to pull in different directions all at the same time: so much so that her eyes appeared where a mouth could be expected, and her fish-like lips spread elsewhere. Gawain was a brave knight of stout constitution, and Arthur needed an answer… so he nodded his agreement to the marriage. The hag told him: sovereignty. Women, she proudly announced, most desire to choose their own destiny and be not ruled by men.

This was not an answer that Arthur had previously heard, so he thanked her and went on his way. Arriving at Gromer Somer Joure's castle, Arthur first delivered the many ideas accrued over the year. This was fruitless … wise men were clearly not wise about women. Gromer tired of Arthur's list and drew his sword. The king had one last answer to try – that given to him by the crone – and he offered this to the huge knight advancing blade-first towards him.

Gromer stopped, sword mid-swing, and then lowered the blade placidly; Arthur had solved the riddle. A knight of his word, Gromer spared Arthur's life and gestured to the king to leave.

Returning to Camelot, the old hag was waiting for Arthur and introduced herself as Lady Ragnell. Arthur took her to meet Gawain, and broke the news as gently as he could; Ragnell prettied herself by wiping the drool from her face. Gawain, brave Gawain, looked aghast but announced that he was relieved

Count des Broches fights against King Nabor and Gawain, from *Romance of Lancelot of the Lake*, 1344. It was not unusual for the Order of the Round Table to fight on opposing sides in friendly tournaments, and Gawain was a highly sought-after warrior. (Alamy)

for Arthur's safety and indebted to the lady for saving his king, so much so that he would marry her even if she was a fiend so foul as the devil himself.

Ragnell flashed her brown teeth in a smile of sorts and the wedding was organized. Gawain upheld the brave and courteous traditions of the Order of the Round Table throughout the ceremony and without flinching kissed his ogre of a bride in front of a horrified congregation. He led her by the hand to their wedding feast, where Ragnell proceeded to devour several large, roasted hogs. Her belching made the tables shudder and lifted tapestries from the walls. Gawain, Arthur, and a handful of the most chivalrous knights treated Ragnell as a lady, but inwardly they all felt the revulsion shown outwardly by other guests at the feast.

Gawain had been secretly dreading the end of the feast but once again led his wife by the hand… this time into their bedchamber. Gawain could hardly look at Ragnell as she wrenched at her ill-fitting gown, but she reminded him of his duty as a husband, and of the oath he had sworn to serve Arthur. Summoning up his courage for king and country, Gawain embraced Ragnell; but she felt different. He cautiously opened one eye and saw that he held not the monster he had married, but a woman more beautiful than any he had seen before.

Ragnell explained that this was her true form; her stepmother was an evil sorceress who had transformed her into a vile hag as a curse. She told Gawain

PERCEVAL

Perceval (also known as: Parsifal; Percivale; Peredur; sometimes named as a son of Gawain but more often the son of King Pellinor) was the original hero of the Grail Quest according to Chrétien de Troyes' *Perceval* and the authors who completed the story after Chrétien's death. He was raised by his mother in the wilds of Wales, unaware of knights and chivalry until he first laid eyes on a knight. From that day, he determined to himself to become a knight and travelled to Camelot, proving to be one of Arthur's greatest knights. After the Grail Quest ended, Perceval took up holy orders.

Perceval continues to appear as an important character in Arthurian legend after his introduction by Chrétien and is a popular character in medieval European stories, but the Vulgate Cycle and Malory's renderings of the Grail Quest cast Galahad as the ultimate hero, relegating Perceval to a supporting role. In Welsh legend, he is named Peredur, tentatively identified as a quasi-historical northern British leader from the post-Roman period.

that this bespelling meant that she could keep her true, radiant appearance either by night as he lay with her or by day when she accompanied him around Camelot … but never both.

Gawain needed to decide: should he see her beauty at night, by himself, or worry more about how others at Camelot perceived himself and his wife? Noble as ever, Gawain decided that the decision was not his to make, instead asking Ragnell: 'Which would you choose, my lady?'

By asking her to choose for herself, Gawain had offered Ragnell that which women most desired: sovereignty. Granting her the right to decide her own mind broke the curse altogether, so that Lady Ragnell would never again appear as an old hag with the stature of a swollen toad and the oddly placed lips of a fish. Gawain's honourable behaviour towards his wife, and his loyal gesture of marriage on behalf of his king, meant that he went to bed a happy and relieved man and happily strode out with his beautiful new wife when morning came.

* * *

The loathly lady was a literary device popular in a number of medieval stories. The tale told here is based on the 15th-century *The Wedding of Sir Gawain and*

'Sir Gawaine the Son of Lot, King of Orkney.' By Howard Pyle.

The Winchester Round Table

A magnificent Round Table hangs in the Great Hall at Winchester (Hampshire, England); it weighs more than a ton and has a diameter of nearly 20 feet. The table is believed to have been built during the reign of Edward I in the 13th century for a tournament celebrating the engagement of one of Edward's daughters; the décor as seen today was added in the reign of Henry VIII in the 16th century and includes a Tudor rose. The Winchester Round Table places the king and 24 knights around it, and includes a portrait of King Arthur.

This grand Round Table hangs in the Great Hall of Winchester castle. It was possibly built in the reign of Edward I (1272–1307). (Alamy)

Lady Ragnell, which did not appear in Malory's *Le Morte Darthur*. The surprisingly modern and humorous plot can also be read in Geoffrey Chaucer's 'The Wife of Bath's Tale' from his *Canterbury Tales*, John Gower's 'Tale of Florent', and the 18th-century 'The Marriage of Sir Gawain' as reinterpreted by Bishop Thomas Percy. A modern parallel may be drawn to Dreamworks Pictures' animated fantasy movie *Shrek* (2001).

In some versions of the adventure Ragnell gives birth to a son of Gawain's named Gingalain or Gyngolyn (originally written by Renaut de Beaujeu as *Le Bel Inconnu* or *The Fair Unknown*); Roger Lancelyn Green's version names the child as Perceval, who became one of the Knights of the Round Table and a hero in the Grail Quest.

Ragnell lived with Gawain for seven years but then disappeared from Camelot forever: possibly to bring Perceval up uncorrupted by courtly life. The role of the evil stepmother is on occasion recast as Morgan Le Fay, Arthur's half-sister and rival.

Erec and Enide

Guinevere's expression was one of shock: never before had a mere dwarf felt it appropriate to reprimand the Queen of Logres. She was riding with a small group of courtiers, when the vile little man, who rode beside a knight clad in beautiful blue and gold armour and an elegant lady, had ridden forward ordering the party from Camelot to clear the way for his lord and lady. He slashed at one of Guinevere's maids with a barbed whip as he pushed his mule into the royal crowd, and cursed at the queen when she stood her ground.

Erec, a young squire who had spent three uneventful years at Arthur's court, also felt the truculent little man's whip tear across his face when he attempted to intervene in defence of Guinevere. Incensed by the horrible little rogue's behaviour and sensing his chance to prove his worth to the king, the unarmed Erec galloped in pursuit when the dwarf and his companions rode on without pause.

Hartmann von Aue was a Swabian German knight and poet, who authored *Erek* and *Iwein*. This late 13th-century miniature shows his coat of arms. (Alamy)

Following the three riders into a walled citadel where the blue and gold knight was receiving an exalted welcome, Erec rode through the streets anonymously and found lodging for the evening with a poor yet honourable old knight and his daughter. Although she was dressed in a meagre gown, the daughter was wonderfully pretty, and she blushed when she noticed Erec staring at her, such was her purity. He fell in love with her at that moment; her name was Enide.

Awed by Enide's beauty, Erec was immediately presented with a chivalrous way to win her affection: the very next day, his host explained, a tournament was to be fought outside the citadel. The prize was a sparrowhawk, which the winner would carry from its silver perch to present to his chosen lady. Knights travelled from across Logres to take part, but one knight had triumphed in the previous two tournaments and had declared that he intended to fight again and present the hawk to his lady; the townsfolk already called him the Knight of the Sparrowhawk. This knight, a great warrior named Yder, had been cheered into the citadel earlier that day, wearing his splendid blue and gold armour and accompanied by a lady and his mean-spirited dwarf. Erec realized that by winning the tournament, he could declare his love for Enide and defend Guinevere's honour together as one.

In armour borrowed from the old knight, Erec rode out the next morning with Enide beside him. Yder's dwarf trotted around on his mule, mocking Erec and every other knight who attended the tournament. Every other knight declined to fight against Yder, such was his warlike reputation and his dwarf's vocal derision, but Erec came to blows with the blue and gold knight. The pair fought first from horseback, and when their horses fell dead they drew swords and hacked away each other's armour. They duelled all day and as night approached both knights were weak from spilled blood; Erec fought in a fury, remembering the dwarf's insult to Guinevere and his whipped face, and as Yder's blade drove into his thigh, he felled his opponent by carving his own blade through the blue and gold knight's shoulder. Erec then split Yder's helmet in two, exposing his enemy's skullbone; leaping forward to unlace the wounded knight's helmet to remove his head properly, Erec paused as Yder begged for mercy. This was a tournament, not a fight to the death, so Erec regained his composure and sent Yder to beg for Guinevere's mercy. The vulgar dwarf slunk away before Erec could find him. Triumphantly presenting the sparrowhawk to the blushing Enide, Erec found his gift accepted and they married soon after; Guinevere rewarded Erec's deeds by making him a Knight of the Round Table.

Erec lived to please Enide; he could not bear to be apart from her, and in a short space of time he no longer found time for jousting, tournaments, or questing. All he wished to do was spend time with his beloved wife, and shunned his knightly duties to do so. Whispered stories spread around Camelot about this knight who would not quest, and Enide came to hear of them. Embarrassed by her husband's reputation, and upset that the whisperers blamed her for distracting Erec, she confronted him about his lack of adventure, and told him that he must act more like the brave knight she had first met. Erec's reaction was instantaneous: upset that she doubted his valour,

Courtly Love

Courtly love is a key plot device in many Arthurian romances. This emotion mirrored the loyal and devoted relationship between a knight and his lord, but was enacted between a knight and a lady. The knight's love for his lady inspired him to accomplish great deeds in order to win her favour; the knight's motives were not necessarily sexual, and on occasion the lady in question was unaware of the knight's devotion as courtly love was sometimes pursued secretly. Ladies, in return, could offer a token of their affection to a knight at tournament (such as a ribbon to hang from the knight's lance), regardless of their own marital status. The tales of Erec and Yvain explore courtly love, as does the rather more amorous evolution of Lancelot and Guinevere's love.

he told her to mount her horse and ride out with him… he would prove himself and his wife would witness him doing so.

Erec armed himself for adventure, and departed from the gates of Camelot alongside Enide. He requested that she would ride ahead of him, and would not speak to him unless he first spoke to her. He wanted Enide to see his deeds of redemption, and wanted to be by her side as always, but he needed to prove his honour unaided. Saddened that they would not speak, and fearing what might happen on their adventure, Enide nevertheless obeyed and rode ahead into the forest beyond Camelot's walls.

'Geraint rode in silence.' By TH Robinson. Erec and Geraint are one and the same character: Chrétien de Troyes' original tale named the hero as Erec and Welsh legend named him as Geraint.

Through the cool, shaded forest their horses took them. Enide did not speak, and Erec rode some distance behind her. As they crossed a gently bubbling stream, three roguish robber knights charged out from the shadows, heading towards Enide intent on stealing her horse. Enide cried out in alarm to Erec, and he spurred his horse into action, knocking the first of the false knights from his saddle. Erec whirled about and sent the second knight sprawling to the floor with a heavy wound, and upon seeing this the third knight turned his own horse about and started to ride off. Erec gave chase for only a few moments before catching up and delivering a mighty blow that felled the final villain. The three knights scuttled away into the undergrowth, well beaten. Turning to Enide, Erec pardoned her this once for having spoken her warning, and asked her to lead the three knights' horses as a prize.

As they travelled through the countryside in silence, five riders approached. Enide, riding ahead of Erec, realized that these were five more knights intent on attacking them. She turned in her saddle and called out a warning to Erec. He launched his horse at the first of the five; this opponent fell from his saddle wounded by Erec's ferocious assault. The second and third knights' helmets and skulls were cleaved into halves by Erec's deft swordplay, and the fourth and fifth turned their horses about and began to flee. Once more, Erec gave chase and knocked the fourth knight from his horse, cutting him down when he stood his ground before the mounted Erec. As the fourth knight slumped to the ground, the fifth rapidly dismounted and surrendered. The danger past,

Erec once more chastised Enide for calling out to him, but once more forgave her. She now led eight horses but Erec insisted that they must press on to allow him to properly prove his honour.

Journeying deep into the old, untamed forest the knight and lady took shelter at an imposing castle, dining that night with the castle's lord. In return, they gifted him the horses they had won. This lord watched Enide eagerly, noticing for himself her beauty and feeling the same desire that had attracted Erec the very first time he had met her. Asking to speak to her in private, the lord asked Enide to marry him; when she rejected him – for she still truly loved Erec – the lord threatened to kill Erec unless Enide accepted. Fearing for her love's life, Enide agreed. But Enide's beauty was matched by her quick thinking; she told the lord that to keep her honour intact, he must pretend the next morning to abduct her and kill Erec in the process. The lord agreed, and allowed his guests to retire to their bedchamber.

That night, Enide explained to Erec what had happened. They left the castle quickly and quietly, and only when they had gone did the lord realize that Enide had fooled him. In a fury he rode out with one hundred of his horsemen to track them down, remove the head from Erec's shoulders, and forcibly take his wife-to-be. As they closed in on the fugitives, Enide called out a warning to Erec: the strength of his sword arm allowed them to cut through the horsemen and ride to safety, leaving the wounded, and by now humiliated, lord to retreat to his castle. Erec once again forgave Enide, as he now realized that she shouted her warnings only because she wanted no harm to touch him.

Erec and Enide now rode together through the forest, side by side. They talked as they rode, but their conversation was interrupted by a scream. Erec asked Enide to dismount and wait for him away from the unknown danger, and spurred his horse forward. He met a tearful, trembling maiden who explained that two giants had captured her lover and were torturing him. Erec charged ahead with such speed that he almost collided with two foul ogres, standing at twice the height of a fighting man. They brandished whips and clubs, and were using them brutally against a knight they had hanged

Alfred Lord Tennyson

Tennyson was a British Poet Laureate who wrote a series of Arthurian pieces during the Victorian period (an era which saw a resurgence of interest in Arthuriana). Collectively his works are known as *Idylls of the King*, and include 'Gareth and Lynette', 'The Marriage of Geraint', 'Geraint and Enid', 'Balin and Balen', 'Lancelot and Elaine', 'The Holy Grail', and 'The Passing of Arthur'. At an earlier date, he created several shorter poems with Arthurian themes, including 'The Lady of Shalott' and 'Sir Galahad'. Broadly based around Malory's *Le Morte Darthur* and the Welsh *Mabinogion*, Tennyson altered plots to suit his Victorian audience, and as such his contribution to Arthurian literature is far greater than a simple retelling of medieval tales.

from a tree. Ignoring Erec's demand to release the injured knight, they continued to whip him. Charging at them, the first giant battered Erec's horse with his club and stabbed at him with a sword, sending the knight sprawling from the dead horse's saddle with a savage cut to his stomach. Springing to his feet, the wounded Erec plunged his broken lance through the eye of one of the giants, who dropped dead. He cleaved the second in two with a powerful blow from his sword. Freeing the captured knight, Erec ran back through the forest to where he had left Enide, wishing to spend no longer apart from her than was absolutely necessary.

Erec and Yder fight a bitter duel to establish which of them will win the sparrowhawk prize for his lady. By C Walter Hodges.

As he approached Enide, his wound split open and Erec fell to the ground, his innards becoming outtards. Enide ran to his aid, but fainted over his body. As she came to in the now silent forest, Enide was sure that Erec had died, and she took his sharp sword intending to kill herself rather than live without him. But before she could do so, a troop of knights rode past. Dismounting, they removed the sword from Enide's hands, and the lord who rode at the head of the troop offered to bury Erec and marry Enide: once again, her beauty had enthralled a knight upon his very first gaze. Refusing his help, and determined to end her life, she ushered the lord and his knights away. Ignoring her wishes, the lord placed Enide on a horse and gathered up Erec's body, determined to bury the brave knight and marry the beautiful lady.

At the lord's castle, Enide refused to eat or drink. And she refused to marry him. Angry at her discourtesy and overcome with passion, he slapped her across the face. As Enide exclaimed that she would never marry him, for she loved the dead Erec, he hit her again.

But Erec was not dead. The sound of Enide's cries roused him from unconsciousness, and he staggered groggily to his feet. Holding his bleeding wound together with his hand, he stumbled into the castle's hall, picked up a sword, and cut the abusive lord's head from his shoulders. The castle's knights, ladies, and servants all fled in panic, supposing that Erec had risen from death and was a demon from beyond the grave. Enide embraced him.

His wound bound, they rode back to Camelot through the night, each having redeemed themselves to the other: Erec vowed to continue to act as an honourable knight, and Enide would never need to doubt this again.

* * *

Two versions of the story of Erec (also known as: Geraint; Guerec) exist: Chrétien de Troyes' romance *Érec et Énide* written around 1160–70, and the Welsh folktale *Geraint: Son of Erbin* or *Geraint and Enid. Érec et Énide* is the earliest surviving Arthurian romance written by Chrétien de Troyes, and is one of three of his stories for which similar Welsh tales exist (Yvain/Owain and Perceval/Peredur being the others); it seems most likely that the Welsh tales were reworked from Chrétien's original stories, although it is possible that all three were originally Welsh or (more likely) Breton tales adapted by the Frenchman.

In both versions, Erec (or Geraint) wins the sparrowhawk tournament, and the hero forgets to fulfil his knightly duties as he revels in marital bliss. In the Welsh tale, Enid laments that she is the cause of her husband's dishonour, and Geraint believes his wife to have been unfaithful, taking her on an adventure in which he proves his honour and she her fidelity. In Chrétien's version, Enide tells Erec of the talk of the court about his failure to fulfil his duties as a knight, and he once again rides out with her. Both versions end with the lovers' differences resolved.

The late 12th-century German writer Hartmann von Aue's *Erek* and the 13th- century Icelandic *Erex* both evolved from Chrétien de Troyes' tale. In the Victorian age, the poet Tennyson was inspired by the Welsh tale to write the poem 'Enid', which he later expanded upon as the two-part 'Geraint and Enid'. Neither Erec nor Geraint feature strongly in other medieval Arthurian tales, and they do not meaningfully bother the pages of Malory's work.

Tristan and Isolde

Tristan was to become a famous Knight of the Round Table, one of Arthur's greatest knights. Yet he found fame before ever setting foot inside Camelot, as the champion of King Mark of Cornwall.

Tristan was Mark's nephew, and was a young man equally renowned for his skill with a sword blade as he was for his ability with a harp. Mark summoned him to his Great Hall one morning in need of that first prowess: the barbaric and bellicose King Anguish of Ireland had demanded his annual tribute of gold from Mark, but this year the Cornishman did not intend to pay. Anguish had threatened to send an army of howling Irish pirates to raid the Kernow peninsula if cartloads of gold were not sent to him, but Mark's response had been to challenge Anguish. An Irish champion named Marhault – himself a Knight of the Round Table and the brother in law of Anguish – had set sail from the southern shores of the Irish king's realm. Mark's challenge was a shrewd move: instead of an invading army laying waste to his entire lands, the greatest warrior from each kingdom would clash in battle over the king's tribute.

Tristan prepared himself for the coming fight. Marhault, being a servant of Arthur as well as the champion of Anguish, would be a formidable opponent. Many lesser knights would have shirked their duty and declined to fight such

Tristan (James Franco) and Isolde (Sophia Myles) embrace in the 2006 movie *Tristan and Isolde*. (Alamy)

a warrior, but Tristan desired to serve his uncle well. He rode from Mark's hall to meet the Irish ship.

Marhault waited on the beach fully armed; in the hazy morning sun, Tristan could see that the Irishman's helmet and armour were old fashioned – the men of Ireland were not always so well-equipped as knights of Logres – but he also sensed that before him stood an experienced warrior worthy of respect. As was the custom of Cornwall, the combatants were ferried to a tiny island off the coast, big enough for two men to manoeuvre in a duel but no larger than that.

Both knights touched blades and the duel began. With his first blow, Marhault's Irish axe cut into Tristan's thigh, slicing through his mail armour and drawing blood. It was not a terrible wound and the Cornishman fought on, dexterously skipping away from Marhault's sharp blade time and again. Tristan's sword fell repeatedly on his opponent's shield, relentlessly hammering on its face. The two knights clashed throughout the morning, the tiny island allowing neither any breathing space. Marhault was a superb axeman, but Tristan's dancing agility prevented the seasoned warrior from landing any further blows. Both men began to tire; as their arms became heavy with exertion it was usual for the duellists to step back and catch their breath, but the seawater lapping around the island's edge prevented either from doing so. The exhausted Marhault stumbled, and Tristan delivered a mighty blow to the Irishman's helmet, slicing through the iron and snapping his sharp blade as it cut into the skullbone. Marhault fell, unconscious, and Tristan, realizing that blood oozed from his single wound, collapsed moments later.

'How La Beale Isoud nursed Sir Tristram.' By Aubrey Beardsley.

A boat collected both men and Marhault was returned to Ireland for his savage wound to be healed. Tristan had fulfilled his champion's duty. King Mark would not pay any tribute this year.

Tristan's wound was attended by Mark's wise man. He realized that Marhault's axe had been envenomed with a dreadful poison, and that the single wound inflicted on Tristan might well end his life. The solution, he explained, was to send Tristan to Ireland, as only those who had mixed the poison could prepare the cure. Tristan was placed in a ship and washed up anonymously on the shores of Anguish's kingdom.

ARTHURIAN HERALDRY

Although various coats-of-arms have been created for the Knights of the Round Table, there was little formal heraldry associated with these fictitious characters in the earliest medieval stories. Tristan often appeared with a lion, but German artwork preferred to show him with a boar and some more modern designs focus on his harp; the background colour of Tristan's arms varies but is usually *vert* (green). Gawain was often depicted as carrying the arms of Orkney (a double-headed eagle), but the poem *Gawain and the Green Knight* describes an *or* (yellow) pentangle on a *gules* (red) background, and on some occasions he carried the heraldry attributed to Tristan in this book: an *or* (yellow) lion on a *vert* (green) background. Yvain also carried a lion, although whether this was due to his fame as The Knight of the Lion or a hereditary right is difficult to determine.

However, the arms of some knights stabilized quite rapidly into their traditional form: Lancelot, for example, was often shown from the early 13th century onwards with an *argent* (white) shield bearing three *bends gules* (red stripes), although sometimes with only one or two *bends*. Yet disguised in his first appearance in Arthurian literature, in *Le Chevalier de la Charrette*, he carries a plain red shield.

The coats-of-arms used in this book's colour plates are compiled where possible from a 15th-century French manuscript known as *D'Armagnac Armoral* or *La Forme Quon Tenoit Des Torynoys*, and on Jean Froissart's *Meliador* written in the 1380s.

Unknown to the court of Cornwall, Marhault had died from the head wound only days after returning, and his sister – Anguish's queen – had sworn to avenge his death. She removed the broken sword blade from his skull and kept it so that she would never forget her brother's pain. Yet Tristan, unknown in Ireland as Marhault's slayer, had been found half-dead in his ship and taken into Anguish's castle to be healed. Now he lay behind the same castle walls as the queen.

Tristan was healed by Anguish's daughter Isolde; she had not mixed the poison but was a deft healer and tended him day and night. Slowly the wounded knight recovered, and began to play a harp every day to entertain the Irish court. during his recovery he told Isolde that he was a wandering bard named Tantris (a play on his real name) who had been attacked and poisoned. In this guise, he charmed Anguish's followers with songs of melodious beauty, and by the time his strength had fully returned, he was a welcome member of the Irish court. But the queen did not trust him; in secret, she took his sword and compared it to the shard from Marhault's skull, inevitably matching the two pieces together.

Before the vengeful queen could act, Isolde warned Tristan of the danger and helped him to flee to the coast, from where he returned to Mark's castle in Cornwall. She had placed Tristan's life above her duty as a princess, so fond had she grown of him, and as he sailed back across the sea Tristan realized that he had fallen in love with the Irish princess.

Returning to Mark fully healed, Tristan told his story, and dwelt for many hours on the allure of Isolde. Mark was overjoyed that his nephew had returned alive, and in a buoyant flourish decided that this delightful

(OVERLEAF)
Duelling on a tiny island, Tristan eventually overcomes the Irish champion Marhault, breaking his sword as he cleaves through the Irishman's helmet to deliver the winning blow. The Irishman's helmet is antiquated, and his mail lacks *ailettes* (heraldic shoulder plates popular *c.* 1250–1350), but he is still a formidable opponent: Tristan's thigh has been cut by Marhault's poisoned axe. Both duellists' coats of arms are based on *D'Armagnac Armoral.*

Irish princess would be a wonderful queen for Cornwall. A beautiful wife, a healer, and a unification of Cornwall and Ireland that would end his annual tribute … Tristan was stunned when Mark demanded that he immediately return to Ireland to bring Isolde to the Cornish king.

Unsure of how to proceed once he had landed – a friendly welcome being most unlikely – Tristan's solution presented itself to him when the local Irish fisherfolk told him that a dragon was laying waste to Anguish's realm. Seizing this opportunity to allow his reappearance at Anguish's castle, Tristan tracked down the dragon across the blackened, smouldering remains of Ireland. Meeting the old wyrm in battle, the Cornish knight fought bravely: using his shield to beat away the scaly creature's huge talons and dancing sideways to avoid its fiery breath, he eventually plunged his sword deep into the huge beast's throat. Standing astride the neck, Tristan cut the dragon's head from its body and arrived at the court of Anguish to tell of his deed.

'Belle Isoult and Sir Tristram drink the love draught.' By Howard Pyle.

The death of Marhault was forgiven by Anguish when Tristan presented the dragon's head. After all, the duel had been fought honourably – Tristan wisely decided not to remind the Irish king about the poisoned Irish blade – and the dragon had caused carnage greater than any in living memory. Wedding gifts from Mark were presented to Anguish, and shortly afterwards Isolde accompanied Tristan back to his ship. Knight and lady were accompanied by Isolde's servant Bragwaine. She carried a flagon of magical liquid, a love potion for Isolde to drink before she met Mark: King Anguish wanted to be sure that the wedding would be a happy one, and more importantly a profitable one for his kingdom.

Tristan put aside all thoughts of his love for Isolde: he served King Mark, and would carry out his king's command. Isolde knew that her duty as a princess was to seal the bond between two kingdoms by marriage, so she cast aside her feelings for Tristan. Neither spoke of their love as the ship set sail.

On the journey, the travellers grew thirsty. Tristan picked up one of the many flagons on board and poured a glass for each of them. As they drank, their world changed. The hapless Bragwaine had placed the love potion beside the wine and water flagons, and Tristan and Isolde's passion was magically bound forever more.

Despite this Isolde married Mark, sealing an alliance between Cornwall and Ireland. But the new queen met in secret each evening with Tristan. The love potion held so strong an enchantment over them that they could not stop themselves, despite their attempted loyalty to Mark, and the king was outraged when he discovered their liaisons. A petty little dwarf named Frocin one day saw a bloodstain on the queen's sheets, and recognized that it came from the old wound inflicted on Tristan by Marhault. In a maddened rage, Mark attacked Tristan with a sword, but the older man could not lay a blow on his agile champion. The lovers fled from Mark's castle and lived together in the forest, away from the eyes of Mark's warriors.

But Mark wanted Isolde returned to ensure that his alliance with Anguish held firm, and because he could not bear the thought of Tristan lying beside his queen. Offering a truce to Isolde, Mark announced that she could return to his castle so long as Tristan never laid eyes on her again. Faced with a life in exile living under a canopy of trees, the lovers agreed that they must part. Isolde returned to Mark, and Tristan travelled to Arthur's court at Camelot to serve the great King of Logres.

'Sir Tristram.' By Howard Pyle.

Isolde lived unhappily while Tristan flourished. The knight was awarded Marhault's vacant seat at the Round Table, and quested far and wide in Arthur's name. He met a Breton maiden who shared the name of his true love, and married Isolde the White shortly afterwards. He married her for his love of her name rather than through any affection for the lady.

Gravely wounded in battle on a quest for Arthur, Tristan was carried back to his Breton castle. Knowing that his life was draining from his body, he sent a ship to find his true love Isolde, asking that she attend his wounds and that they be united just once more. Tristan asked that a signal be made when the ship returned: if the sails were black Isolde had refused to come, if they were white his love had returned to him. As he lay gravely ill, he asked his wife Isolde the White what colour the sails were when the ship landed. She had learned of his request and of his signal, and her jealousy led her to say that the sails were black. Hearing this, Tristan died of despair. Isolde stepped from the white-sailed ship and ran to Tristan's chamber. Seeing his body on the bed, she killed herself at his side.

The lovers lay beside one another in death. From Tristan's grave rose a vine, and from Isolde's a rose: as time passed, the vine and rose became intertwined and the lovers were together once more.

* * *

The story of Tristan (also known as: Tristram; Tristrem; Drystan) and Isolde (or Iseult) was one of the most influential of medieval romances, presenting a perfect love triangle between king, loyal champion, and dutiful queen, and a love potion plot that contributes an almost fairy tale ambience. Tristan existed as a medieval hero before being drawn into Arthurian legend; the story of Tristan and Isolde stands alone without any reference to Arthur's court or the Round Table being necessary, but drawing this tale into an Arthurian context emphasized the importance and significance of Tristan as a knight. It was not unknown for other Knights of the Round Table to be drawn from standalone tales into Arthur's court.

Two strands of Tristan's legend evolved in the medieval period, possibly predated by now-lost Breton or Welsh folklore. The 13th-century *Prose Tristan* was the first story to place the hero in an Arthurian context. Before this, in the late 12th century, the French writers Thomas and Béroul contributed now-incomplete Tristan romances, and it is likely that Chrétien de Troyes wrote a Tristan story that is now completely lost (tentatively entitled *Mark and Iseut la Blonde*). Tristan was also a popular hero with medieval German and Scandinavian authors, including Gottfried von Strassburg and Eilhart von Oberge.

In Malory's *Le Morte Darthur*, Tristan is one of the most regularly featured heroes in the book, although Malory's version of *Tristan and Isolde* ends with Tristan being slain by the jealous and furious Mark as he plays his harp for Isolde. The vignette of the black and white sails that more frequently ends the tale is also known in, and probably incorporated from, the Classical Greek myth of Theseus.

YVAIN: THE KNIGHT OF THE FOUNTAIN

Arthur, Guinevere, and a handful of knights including Gawain's cousin Yvain gathered around Calogrenant. Calogrenant himself was a cousin of Yvain, and he had arrived earlier that day on an exhausted horse. As was the custom of Camelot he was asked to regale his hosts with a remarkable tale.

The weary knight began his tale by explaining that he had decided to seek out adventure in the wild Forest of Brocéliande, over the sea in Brittany. He knew not whether he had ridden for a day or a week after landing overseas, but chopping his way through the thick forest he eventually chanced upon a castle towering on a rocky headland over a luscious, open valley that echoed with birdsong. Escorted into the castle by beautiful maidens, who repaired his thorn-damaged armour and polished his shield, he was fed and told of an enchanted fountain that sprang up in a glade deep in the forest. It was guarded by the Knight of the Fountain: a red-clad warrior named Esclados who fought against anyone taking its water. This, Calogrenant thought, was the adventure he so sought. Riding to the fountain, he dismounted and, as he had been instructed at the castle, used a small cup beside the fountain to collect water to pour onto the fountain's stone slab. No sooner had the water been poured than a furious storm crashed overhead and the red-clad knight charged towards him and attacked without warning. Calogrenant sheepishly described how the knight easily overpowered him amidst the thunder and lightning, circled around him on his steed, bowed mockingly from his saddle, and rode off. Without drinking from the fountain, Calogrenant fled.

'Sir Ewaine poureth water on the slab.' By Howard Pyle.

A larger crowd gathered as Calogrenant told his story, and excitement buzzed around the Great Hall. Arthur declared that he would

A misericord depicting Yvain's horse trapped in the portcullis of Esclados' castle. A popular scene with medieval audiences, this late 14th-century example is from New College Chapel, Oxford (Bridgeman)

like to see this fountain for himself, little knowing that Yvain had already resolved to undertake the very same trip to avenge his cousin's humiliation.

Yvain set out the next morning. He hoped to defeat the Knight of the Fountain, impressing Arthur and restoring Calogrenant's honour by doing so. Yvain's journey was no more simple than his cousin's had been, but he eventually cut his way through the forest and found the Castle of the Maidens. He received the same welcome as Calogrenant had, and was told the way to the fountain when his armour had been returned to him glinting more than ever before.

The air was still as Yvain approached the fountain. Beside it sat the cup as described by his cousin, and he could see the stone slab onto which he must pour the water. Unlike Calogrenant, Yvain was prepared for what was about to happen. He remained seated on his horse, his shining shield on his shoulder and his sword at the ready. He leaned down and scooped water into the cup, and as he poured it onto the slab, the sky darkened and thunder peeled. Lightning crashed into the forest around him, and surging out of the darkness came the Knight of the Fountain.

Yvain had prepared well: as Esclados charged at him, Yvain dodged his horse to the side and his opponent flew past. As he did so, Yvain chopped down hard with his sword delivering a devastating blow to his attacker. The momentum of the red-clad steed took its rider out of the glade and into the darkness of the forest.

Yvain set out in pursuit, following the bloody trail left by the Knight of the Fountain. Yvain followed closely behind Esclados as he rode towards a castle. The gate was opened and the wounded knight's horse rode in; as Yvain followed, a portcullis fell suddenly and he could do nothing to react. The heavy iron gate fell onto Yvain's horse, cutting it in two. The rear end lay outside the castle's gate, but the front end – and Yvain with it – rolled into the castle's courtyard. His head ringing from the fall, Yvain stood up, sword at the ready, but no-one was to be seen. Leaving his horse either side of the gate, Yvain followed the blood trail.

Morgan Le Fay

Morgan Le Fay (also known as: Morgana; Morgan the Wise) was one of Arthur's half-sisters, who originally was known for aiding his healing on the enchanted Isle of Avalon. However, by the time of the Vulgate Cycle, Morgan's character had changed and she held an obsessive hatred for Arthur due to his father Uther slaying her father Gorlois and then marrying her mother Igraine. Morgan was taught the dark arts of magic by Merlin, including the ability to fly and change shape (the latter showing the Celtic influence on Arthurian magic); she used sorcery to launch attacks on Arthur's power throughout his reign, sometimes being reconciled with the king to attend his journey to Avalon. Married to King Uriens of Gore, Morgan was the mother of Arthur's loyal knight Yvain.

He turned to the sound of footsteps behind him; rather than the guards he expected, he came face to face with a young woman. She introduced herself as Lunete, and politely explained that Esclados, the protector of the fountain and castle, lay mortally wounded and the Lady of the Fountain grieved for him. She led Yvain to a small window looking into a chapel, where he saw Esclados laid out. Beside him stood the most beautiful woman Yvain had ever seen; a whisper from Lunete told him that this was Laudine, the Lady of the Fountain and owner of the castle. He stood transfixed by her elegance and charm before being led to a quiet garden chamber by Lunete.

Each day, Yvain crept to the window and watched Laudine. Without having spoken a word to the Lady of the Fountain, he had fallen in love with her. Lunete brought food and water to him, but one day, amidst tolling bells, she instead brought news: Esclados had died. Without their protector, the castle, the magical fountain, and Laudine herself would perish.

Yvain (on the right) battles against Esclados (on the left, named here as Aschelon) in this early 13th-century fresco from Castello Rodengo, Italy. (Alamy)

Yvain watched the funeral procession with overwhelming remorse. Laudine looked more elegant than ever before, her pale skin enhanced by the darkness of her mourning robe. That was the very moment that Yvain realized that he could marry no other woman.

Lunete's words of warning were in vain to Yvain; he knew that he would be in danger if he revealed himself to the Lady of the Fountain, yet he was insistent that he must do so. Lunete did all she could to help him: she suggested to Laudine that a new Knight of the Fountain must be found to protect them all, and hinted that a Knight of the Round Table – one of Arthur's famous knights – would surely be chivalrous enough to help… if only one could be found.

(PREVIOUS PAGE)
In the wild uplands, Yvain attacks a huge wyrm to rescue a lion from its scaly grasp. The lion will become his trusting and trusted companion from this encounter onwards, assisting his return to his true love: the Lady of the Fountain. Yvain's heraldry is based on *D'Armagnac Armoral.*

Leaving the castle after nightfall, Yvain rode up the following day and asked to speak with the lady of the castle. Explaining that he had just travelled from Arthur's court, he requested Laudine's hospitality. At the feast that followed, she explained to Yvain her need of a champion. Unless the water of the fountain was guarded by a knight, the castle would fall into decline; and if the castle fell into decline, it was Laudine's destiny to follow. Yvain, of course, promptly agreed to ride out as the Knight of the Fountain.

Clad in the red armour of Esclados, Yvain protected the fountain but treated his defeated foes with honour. Over time, and with Lunete's guidance, he won the heart of Laudine and they married in a joyous ceremony. For three years, Yvain thrived in his role as guardian of the fountain and castle.

And then one day, a band of horsemen crashed through the Forest of Brocéliande. Calogrenant had urged Arthur to send his warriors to find and avenge Yvain – whom all assumed dead – and Arthur himself led his knights, so keen was he to see the mysterious fountain. Riding on from the Castle of the Maidens, they reached the clearing where the fountain stood, and Arthur's stepbrother Kay asked the honour of pouring the water.

As Kay did so, the sky darkened and thunder peeled. Lightning crashed into the forest around him, and surging out of the darkness came the Knight of the Fountain. Wearing the red armour of Esclados, none of Arthur's knights recognized Yvain. And so intent on fulfilling his duty was Yvain that he did not stop to recognize Arthur or his knights.

'Sir Gawaine, Knight of the Fountain.' By Howard Pyle. In a rare slip, the caption should actually name Yvain – Ewaine as Pyle styled him – but instead mistakenly reads Gawaine.

As Kay and the Knight of the Fountain charged each other, Kay was struck such a mighty blow that he somersaulted from his saddle and lay stunned on the earth. Next Arthur sent forward Gawain, the mightiest of his warriors and cousin of Yvain, and he battled for hours against the red-clad knight. Eventually, with horses lying dead, lances broken, shields split in two, and sword blades dulled, Yvain's strength gave way and Gawain was victorious. Removing his stricken opponent's helmet, Gawain was speechless as he came face-to-face with his cousin.

Arthur and Gawain were told Yvain's wonderful story. As they spoke, Yvain felt a growing desire to return to Camelot to serve his king once more, and he explained to Laudine that he must attend both his lady and his king. As Yvain departed with Arthur's knights, Laudine took him to one side and

CHRÉTIEN DE TROYES

Although earlier writers such as Geoffrey of Monmouth created the medieval legend of King Arthur as we know it today, Chrétien de Troyes switched the emphasis of Arthurian literature from the actions of the king to the deeds of his knights.

We know very little of Chrétien, except that he wrote in France in the late 12th century. He added five major stories to Arthurian legend (and possibly others, including a now lost tale about Tristan and Isolde). Chrétien's contributions were: *Érec et Énide*, *Yvain: Le Chevalier au Lion*, *Le Chevalier de la Charrette*, *Cligés*, and *Perceval: Le Conte du Graal*. The latter was unfinished by Chrétien when he died around 1181; later writers continued where he left off and these tales are known as the Grail Continuations.

As noted in some of the stories in this book, Chrétien may have been heavily influenced by Breton or Welsh folklore, although it is equally possible that writers in those cultures reworked his ideas at a later date for their regional audiences.

Chrétien developed the idea of courtly love, and emphasized chivalry as the ideal quality for an aspiring knight. It was also he who introduced to the legend Camelot as the name of Arthur's castle, along with the most renowned of all Arthurian knights: Lancelot. In introducing Lancelot, Chrétien was the first writer to explore the love triangle between Arthur, Guinevere, and Lancelot.

gave him a ring. This ring, she said, was a symbol of their love and he must wear it every day. She also told him that he should adventure with the Order of the Round Table for one year, but must prove his love for her by returning a year to that very day. Yvain swore that he would do so.

Such was Yvain's delight of life at the Round Table that he carelessly forgot his vow to his lady and remained at Camelot for well over a year. He accomplished many brave feats in the name of Arthur, and thoughts of Laudine and the fountain seldom entered his head… until one day a maiden arrived from Brocéliande. She announced that Laudine demanded the return of her ring, for Yvain did not deserve the honour of wearing it.

This news was too much for Yvain to bear; he had failed his lady even though he faithfully served his king. Fleeing Camelot, he ran mad in the woods and forests of Logres, eschewing clothing and barking at the moon, until eventually nursed back to health by a wise-woman. Donning his armour once again, he resolved to win back Laudine's love through virtuous adventuring as a knight.

Riding through a devastated area of craggy upland, Yvain crested a hill and was confronted with the rarest of sights: a drake, an old wyrm of Logres, a huge serpent that had laid waste to the surrounding realm. Constricted within its powerful coils was a lion, bravely fighting for its life. Without thought for his own safety, Yvain threw himself from his horse and charged into the fray, laying about the serpent with his sword. Between the lion's claws and Yvain's shining blade, the serpent fell dead after a struggle that lasted until the sun disappeared. The gallant knight nursed the lion back to health, and it followed him as he departed for further adventures.

Accompanied by his wildcat companion Yvain became known as the Knight of the Lion, and tales of his victories spread throughout Arthur's realm and overseas. In his quest for Laudine's forgiveness, he battled against false knights, foul creatures, and giants; the kindness shown to him by the servant Lunete was repaid by Yvain when he saved her from being burned alive.

Never leaving his side, the lion fought for Yvain and helped him to win back Laudine's love through his worthy deeds. A triumphant return to the Forest of Brocéliande saw the lovers reunited, and Yvain loyally served his lady to his dying day. The Knight of the Lion once more became known as the Knight of the Fountain.

* * *

Yvain (also known as: Ywain; Iwein; Owain) was the son of King Uriens and Arthur's half-sister and enemy Morgan Le Fay, but he acted as an honourable member of the Order of the Round Table and was one of the earliest knights associated with Arthur (being mentioned in Geoffrey of Monmouth's *Historia Regum Britanniae*). A cousin and close companion to Gawain, Malory's Yvain sided with Arthur in the disastrous civil war and fell in battle fighting for his king.

In some stories, the deeds of individual knights are sometimes assigned to other well-known knights. Andrew Lang's early twentieth-century children's book, *Tales of the Round Table*, describes Percival (not Yvain) saving the lion from a dragon.

Yvain is the hero of Chrétien de Troyes' *Le Chevalier au Lion*, where he is called upon to perform heroic deeds to regain the love of his lady, and continues to feature prominently in the Vulgate Cycle. He was a popular knight in German and Icelandic literature, and the medieval Welsh storybook *Mabinogion* includes a similar tale to Yvain's, entitled *Owain and Lunet*, and it is not clear whether Chrétien was inspired by this story or vice versa (the *Mabinogion* was not written until long after Chrétien's death, but the story may have been known in earlier Welsh or Breton tradition). In Malory's work, Yvain features only in passing, including a story where he is attacked and wounded by King Mark of Cornwall.

The names of Yvain and his father Uriens derive from the late sixth-century British rulers of Rheged, Urien, and Owain, who defended their northern British kingdom against Anglo-Saxon expansion.

Beaumains: The Knight of the Kitchen

No sooner had the young man had arrived at Camelot asking to serve Arthur as a knight than he was put to work in the pungent kitchens by Kay, Arthur's imperious stepbrother and steward. As he had no name, Kay mockingly dubbed him Beaumains: meaning 'fair hands', as befitted such a gentle young man. Instead of using his sword arm to uphold the laws of Arthur, Beaumains' blade was the fish knife he used to gut trout. Kay reminded him of this every day for a year.

'Faugh sir! You smell of ye kitchen.' Linet did not hide her disdain for Beaumains' lowly rank with any subtlety. By HJ Ford.

Not all of Arthur's knights were so unkind to Beaumains. Lancelot understood that the kitchen boy wanted to serve the king with honour, and intervened whenever he witnessed Kay's cruelty. For his part, Kay insisted that the boy was ill-bred and not fit to be a knight, for instead of asking Arthur for armour and a horse he had simply asked for food and lodgings. Despite Kay's constant spite, Beaumains showed himself to be of good manners and temperament and he thrived as one of Camelot's many servants.

A year to the day after Beaumains' arrival, a lady named Linet entered Arthur's Great Hall. Rather distraught, she explained to the king that Castle Perilous – home to her sister Lyonesse – was besieged by a tyrannical knight named Ironside. The very mention of this name caused a sharp intake of breath around the hall: known to many as the Knight of the Red Lands, Ironside was a terrifying beast of a warrior who had captured and slain several of Arthur's knights. Linet begged for help to save her sister. Even the bravest of Arthur's knights paused in silent unease.

Beaumains listened from the back of the hall, a tray of fish in his hands. As Linet asked a second time for a brave knight's aid, he seized the moment. Putting the fish down and stepping forward, he made his own request of Arthur: to be knighted by Lancelot and to accompany Linet to save Lyonesse.

Pleased by the young man's courage, and aware of his patient service in the kitchens, Arthur was delighted to grant Beaumains his request. Linet, repelled by her would-be hero's fishy odour and offended that Arthur sent a mere servant to help her, stormed out of the hall and rode from Camelot.

Beaumains rummaged through Camelot's old armoury and took a rusty mail coat, a musty yellowing surcoat, and a dusty lance. He rode out after Linet, closely followed by Kay and Lancelot. As the poorly clad knight drew alongside Linet's horse, Kay began to mock him once again for the armour he had chosen. Enough was enough. Wheeling his horse about, Beaumains charged straight at Kay with a levelled lance and easily dislodged him from his saddle. Taking Kay's sword, shield, and lance – all so much better than his own – Beaumains saw Lancelot approaching. Lancelot laughed at the sight of Kay miserably grovelling at the tip of his very own lance, and knighted Beaumains. To do so, he needed to know the young man's real name and Beaumains told him: Gareth, a brother of Gawain. He had chosen to arrive at Camelot unknown, so that Arthur would judge him on merit more than on family reputation. He asked that Lancelot would not reveal his identity until he returned. Duly knighted, Gareth set off in pursuit of Linet who had ridden on without looking back.

(OPPOSITE)
Lady Linet explains to the Black Knight that the boy who accompanies her is barely worth fighting against, and is *certainly not* her champion. Beaumains sits atop his horse impassively awaiting combat; he carries an oddment of armour including Kay's shield (based on *D'Armagnac Armoral*). In all of the plates in this book, the costume of unarmoured men and women is based upon late 12th- to early 14th-century British, French, and German dress; the weapons and equipment of most knights are from the middle of the 13th century, although some wear slightly older armour.

When he drew his horse level beside Linet once again, she spoke to him in the same way that Kay had done for the past year. He was common, a coward for charging Kay unawares, and a varlet for stealing Kay's shield and weapons. Nevertheless, Gareth insisted that he would ride with her, no matter how many insults she spat at him. He was a Knight of the Round Table and he would serve his king as well as he could. Linet rode on in silence, never looking at him nor speaking to him.

On the next day, they encountered a knight clad all in black. His black pavilion stood beside a black hawthorn tree, and his black-clad horse was tethered nearby. He called out a challenge to the approaching riders. The Black Knight asked Linet if Gareth was her champion; leaving Gareth behind, she rode up to the Black Knight and explained that he was merely a kitchen boy and no champion of hers. Perhaps, she said, the Black Knight could defeat him and become her champion?

The two knights set their horses at one another; lances crashed onto shields, and both warriors flew from their saddles. Jumping to their feet with swords drawn, they parried each other's wild blows, until Gareth – fighting with the strength of a giant – battered his opponent to the ground. Gareth took his opponent's black armour and black-clad horse, and ordered the knight to journey to Camelot to swear allegiance to Arthur. Linet and Gareth rode on.

'Sir Gareth doeth Battle with the Knight of the River Ford.' By Howard Pyle. Many duels in Arthurian literature take place at a ford, and here Beaumains defeats the Blue Knight in one such fracas.

Linet continued to insult Gareth. She had not heard Gareth announce his true lineage to Lancelot.

On the next day, they encountered a knight clad all in green, waiting beside a green pavilion with a green-clad horse tethered nearby. He called out to the approaching riders, mistaking Gareth for the Black Knight, his brother. Gareth replied that he was not that knight, but had defeated him the previous day. The Green Knight asked Linet if Gareth was her champion; she rode up to the Green Knight and explained that he was merely a kitchen boy and no champion of hers. Perhaps, she said, the Green Knight could defeat him and become her champion?

The two knights set their horses at one another; lances crashed onto shields, and both warriors flew from their saddles. Jumping to their feet with swords drawn, they parried each other's wild blows, until Gareth once more battered his opponent to the ground. Gareth took his opponent's green armour and green-clad horse, and ordered the knight to journey to Camelot to swear allegiance to Arthur. Linet and Gareth rode on. Linet once again mocked Gareth's low status.

The following day, they encountered a knight clad all in red, waiting beside a red pavilion with a red-clad horse tethered nearby. He called out to the approaching riders, mistaking Gareth for the Green Knight, his brother. Gareth replied that he was not that knight, but had defeated him the previous day. The Red Knight asked Linet if Gareth was her champion; she rode up to the Red Knight and explained that he was merely a kitchen boy and no champion of hers. Perhaps, she said, the Red Knight could defeat him and become her champion?

As before, the knights clashed and Gareth defeated his opponent. He took his opponent's red armour and red-clad horse, and ordered the knight to journey to Camelot to swear allegiance to Arthur. Linet and Gareth rode on once more. Linet mocked Gareth as the Knight of the Kitchen, a slayer of trout, and hero to the turnip.

Upon the next morning, they encountered a knight clad all in blue, waiting beside a blue pavilion next to a stream with a blue-clad horse tethered nearby. He called out to the approaching riders, mistaking Gareth for the Red Knight, his brother. Gareth replied that he was not that knight, but had defeated him the previous day. The Blue Knight asked Linet if Gareth was her champion; she rode up to the Blue Knight and explained that he was merely a kitchen boy and no champion of hers. Perhaps, she said, the Blue Knight could defeat him and become her champion?

As with the Blue Knight's three brothers, a duel began. Wild blows were exchanged, until Gareth battered his opponent to the ground. Gareth took his opponent's blue armour and blue-clad horse, and ordered the knight to journey to Camelot to swear allegiance to Arthur. Linet and Gareth rode on in silence.

Castle Perilous came into view early the next day, its towers rising high into the sky. Linet's sister Lyonesse still held out against the encircling horde of Ironside's army. Linet broke her silence to speak to Gareth, explaining that Ironside was renowned for possessing the strength of seven warriors. He had laid siege to the castle in the hope that Arthur's knights would try to relieve it, allowing him to slay yet more Knights of the Round Table. Speaking more kindly than before, for he had served her well over the previous days and never once protested against her insults, Linet told Gareth that if he could defeat Ironside he would surely be known as one of the great knights in Logres.

Riding towards a huge pavilion set some distance from the castle walls, Gareth passed a timeworn tree from which bodies were hanging. He realized that the decaying corpses of some 40 of Arthur's knights swung from nooses, victims of Ironside gruesomely displayed for all to see. Summoning enough courage to ride on, Gareth approached the tent and called out a challenge.

Le Morte Darthur

Written in 15th-century England by a 'knight prisoner', *Le Morte Darthur* is perhaps the ultimate retelling of Arthurian legend. Building on many diverse sources – and substantially reworking or adding some original plots – the author Sir Thomas Malory describes not just the death of Arthur alluded to in the piece's title, but the king's rise to power and the deeds of those knights who served him.

Acting as a collator and translator, Malory most likely wrote his story of 'King Arthur and his Noble Knights of the Round Table' in the 1450s–70s, before it was renamed *Le Morte Darthur* (later corrected to *Le Morte d'Arthur*), then divided into books and chapters, and published by William Caxton in 1485.

Ironside emerged from the pavilion ready for battle. He was a great bear of a warrior, clad in blood-red armour and carrying a massive two-handed sword. His men began to gather around to watch the spectacular death of yet another Knight of the Round Table.

The red-clad knight prepared his horse for combat, and Gareth checked over the Blue Knight's armour that he still wore. As he did so, Linet rode up. She pointed to a window high in one of the castle's towers, and Gareth could see the pretty face of Lyonesse looking down at them.

Taunts flew in Gareth's direction before the duel began, but the blue-clad Knight of the Round Table ignored these insults just as he had done forever before. Knights red and blue levelled their lances and they spurred their horses at one another. Each was thrown from his saddle by the first, tremendous impact, and both then charged at each other with swords in their hands. Ironside's two-handed sword cleaved powerful blows onto Gareth's blue shield, and Gareth fought back with strength and skill. Both knights traded blows that carved away armour and helmets and they fought past noon. Blood flowed freely. Despite Ironside's famous strength, Gareth matched him and the duel hung in the balance. The red and blue knights fought until darkness fell, and they agreed to resume hostilities in the morning.

As Gareth lay down to sleep against the castle wall, he saw Lyonesse gazing down from her window. As their eyes met he instantly fell in love with her, and realized that he must defeat Ironside to win her affection. Rising from slumber, he declared that the fight must continue immediately. With renewed vigour, both knights laid about each other, and Ironside threw Gareth to the ground. Ironside struggled to thrust his great sword into Gareth's torso, and as he did so, Linet cried out in pity. Inspired by this sudden show of concern, the badly wounded Gareth flung his opponent aside and hacked at him until the broken Ironside begged for mercy. He screamed for mercy for those he had killed, and sobbed that he fought only to avenge his brother who had died at the blade of a Knight of the Round Table.

Showing the same calmness that he had displayed when mocked by Kay in the kitchen and Linet as they rode, Gareth accepted the pleas of this cruel

Gareth vanquishes the Knight of the Red Lands while Linet watches from the trees. (Alamy)

man; he forced him to surrender to Lyonesse and swear his loyalty to Arthur. Ironside did both, and was sent to Camelot to seek the king's forgiveness and to reveal to the king Beaumains' true identity.

Linet took Gareth to meet Lyonesse, and he remained at Castle Perilous while his wounds were tended by the sisters. Linet now spoke to him warmly, and Lyonesse returned his affection. As he recovered and gained the ladies' trust, Gareth revealed his true identity to his hosts.

The marriage of Gareth and Lyonesse was announced in no time at all. One evening, Lyonesse told Gareth to sleep in the hall and that she would come to his bed to make love to him; Linet, displeased that the happy

'The Lady Layonnesse cometh to the Pavilion of Sir Gareth.' By Howard Pyle.

couple intended to consummate their love before the wedding, enlisted the assistance of a sorceress. As the lovers lay together, they were surprised by an eerie, shimmering knight who entered the hall and attacked them. As the ghostly warrior raised his sword above the lovers, Gareth lunged for his own blade and deftly beheaded their assailant. In the skirmish, the knight had driven his blade into Gareth's thigh. Gareth fainted and the decapitated body disappeared in a wisp of smoke.

As Gareth recovered the next day, Lyonesse whispered to him once more that she would come to him in the night. And again, as they lay together, the same spectral assassin entered their hall, its head intact. Linet had used an enchanted ointment to bring it back to life. Despite his thigh wound, Gareth rose and beheaded the knight once again. This time, he cut the head into quarters and scattered them into Castle Perilous' moat.

Linet's miraculous ointment was put to use once more, and for a third time, Gareth fended off the otherworldly knight's interruption as he lay with Lyonesse. However, Linet's intervention had the effect she desired, as the very next day Lyonesse and Gareth married with both of them remaining pure before the ceremony.

And as foretold by Linet before his duel with Ironside, the Knight of the Kitchen became one of Arthur's greatest knights.

* * *

Gareth (also known as: Beaumains; Guerrehet) was the youngest son of King Lot and Queen Morgause of Orkney; Morgause was Arthur's hostile half-sister and Lot was a sometime enemy of Arthur, but Gareth served loyally at the Round Table. Gareth was one of the five Brothers of Orkney who served at the Round Table: himself, Gawain, Gaheris, Agravaine, and the infamous Mordred (who was in fact only their half-brother, being born to Arthur and Morgause).

The tale of Beaumains/Gareth seems to have been an original piece of storytelling by Malory, which is unusual as *Le Morte Darthur* generally presents stories first written in the preceding three centuries. However, there are strong links between the story of Gareth and Renaut de Beaujeu's earlier *Le Bel Inconnu* or *The Fair Unknown,* about a knight who arrives at Arthur's court in a similar way and proceeds to journey on a quest with an uncompanionable lady to save her sister (the unknown knight actually being Gawain's son).

Tennyson's poem about Gareth ends with him marrying Linet, rather than her sister, and the coloured knights whom he defeats on his journey are replaced by knights associated with different times of the day. Gareth's patient and courteous behaviour, coupled with his valour as a knight, win over the rather scornful Linet.

Gareth served Arthur until his death close to the end of the king's reign, falling to Lancelot's sword as king and champion fought against one another for Guinevere.

It was not unusual in Arthurian legend for knights to disguise themselves behind unknown heraldry for a variety of reasons. Lancelot and Tristan often hide their true identities during jousts, tournaments, and adventures so that they will be judged on their feats of arms rather than their reputations. At other times, knights withhold their identity to disguise their love of a lady or their fellow knights, and on occasion (such as in *Gawain and the Green Knight*), an enchantment veils a knight.

EPILOGUE: THE FALL OF THE ROUND TABLE

All good times must eventually end. Arthur ruled wisely and fairly for many summers and winters, sending his knights far and wide to uphold honour and chivalry. This they did and Logres flourished.

And then at one great feast, thunder rolled and lightning flashed, and before the Order of the Round Table appeared a vision of the Holy Grail: a revered vessel into which Christ's blood had drained, making it able to cure all ill.

The Round Table, as depicted in *La Queste du Saint Graal et le mort d'Arthus*, c. 1220. (Alamy)

Arthur was inspired by this vision. He sent his knights to seek out the Grail, to bring it to Camelot so that he could use its powers for the good of his kingdom. In this they failed: many knights died in unfamiliar distant lands, others searched fruitlessly and returned to Camelot as broken men, heroes no more. Three of the purest Knights of the Round Table – Perceval, Galahad, and Bors – found the Holy Grail but failed to return with it: Galahad was spirited away to become the Grail's guardian and the others could not touch it.

As the knights adventured far from home searching for the Grail, the kingdom fell into decline. At the end of the Grail Quest, Lancelot and Guinevere's love for one another was revealed by Arthur's nephew treacherous Mordred and this sparked civil war, the like of which had not been seen since Arthur was crowned. The Order of the Round Table split: some knights remained loyal to their king and others sided with Lancelot. As the two forces fought a bitter campaign, Mordred took the crown, removed the Round Table and replaced it with an ostentatious throne for himself.

Arthur led his battered army home to confront Mordred. Almost the last of the Round Table knights died on the pestilent plain where the bloody battle of Camlann was fought, and under stormy skies Mordred and Arthur rained mortal blows onto one other. Only one knight remained, one of the first knights to serve Arthur named Bedivere, and he helped to place his king's mortally wounded body onto a barge. The barge travelled to the faerie Isle of Avalon, where the Lady of the Lake heals Arthur's wounds even to this day. It is said that one day Arthur shall return to rule Logres.

The Order of the Round Table is no more, yet the deeds of its knights shall be remembered for evermore.

SELECTED READING & WATCHING

Some of the older works of literature shown here are available in various editions both old and new; I have listed my preferred or an easily available edition, but many other choices of the same texts are available.

Many older Arthurian texts are available for free online at *The Camelot Project* (d.lib.rochester.edu/camelot-project) and *Internet Sacred Text Archive* (www.sacred-texts.com).

Medieval literature

Anonymous, *The Death of King Arthur* (Faber, 2012) (translated by Simon Armitage)

Anonymous, *Sir Gawain and the Green Knight* (Faber, 2007) (translated by Simon Armitage)

Anonymous, *Sir Gawain and the Green Knight* (Penguin, 2013) (translated by Bernard O'Donoghue)

Anonymous, *Lancelot-Grail* (DS Brewer, 2010) (edited by Norris J Lacy)

Béroul, *The Romance of Tristan* (Penguin, 1970) (translated by Alan S Fedrick)

Chrétien de Troyes, *Arthurian Romances* (Penguin, 1991) (translated by William W Kibler and Carleton W Carroll)

Geoffrey of Monmouth, *The History of the Kings of Britain* (Penguin, 1966) (translated by Lewis Thorpe)

Gottfried von Strassburg, *Tristan* (Penguin, 1967) (translated by AT Hatto)

Robert de Boron, *Merlin and the Grail* (DS Brewer, 2008) (translated by Nigel Bryant)

Sir Thomas Malory, *Le Morte d'Arthur* (Penguin, 1969) (edited by Janet Cowan)

Wace and Layamon, *The Life of King Arthur* (Phoenix, 1997) (edited by Ros Allen and Judith Weiss)

Later literature

Arnold, Matthew, *Tristram and Iseult* (Kessinger, 2010)

Guest, Lady Charlotte, *The Mabinogion* (Oxford University Press, 2007) (translated by Sioned Davies)

Lancelyn Green, Roger, *King Arthur and His Knights of the Round Table* (Puffin, 1953)

Lang, Andrew, *Tales of the Round Table* (Longmans, 1902)

Lanier, Sidney, *The Boy's King Arthur* (Charles Scribner's Sons, 1917)

Matthews, Caitlin and Matthews, John, *The Arthurian Book of Days* (Sidgwick & Jackson, 1990)

Pyle, Howard, *The Story of King Arthur and His Knights* (Charles Scribner's Sons, 1903)

Pyle, Howard, *The Story of the Champions of the Round Table* (Charles Scribner's Sons, 1905)

Pyle, Howard, *The Story of Sir Launcelot and His Companions* (Charles Scribner's Sons, 1907)

Riordan, James, *Tales of King Arthur* (Hamlyn, 1982)

Steinbeck, John, *The Acts of King Arthur and his Noble Knights* (Ballatine Books, 1976)

Tennyson, Alfred, *Idylls of the King* (Arcturus, 2012) (edited by Valerie Purton)

Twain, Mark, *A Connecticut Yankee at King Arthur's Court* (Penguin, 2007)

Reference works

Barber, Richard, *The Arthurian Legends: An Illustrated Anthology* (The Boydell Press, 1979)

Barber, Richard, *King Arthur: Hero and Legend* (The Boydell Press, 1986) (third edition)

Cresswell, Julia, *Legendary Beasts of Britain* (Shire Publications, 2013)

Fulton, Helen (ed.), *A Companion to Arthurian Literature* (Wiley-Blackwell, 2009)

Karr, Phyllis Ann, *The Arthurian Companion* (Chaosium, 2001) (second edition)

Lacy, Norris J and Wilhelm, James J (eds), *The Romance of Arthur* (Routledge, 2012) (third edition)

Lupack, Alan, *The Oxford Guide to Arthurian Literature* (Oxford University Press, 2005)

Mersey, Daniel, *Myths & Legends 4: King Arthur* (Osprey, 2013)

Pearsall, Derek, *Arthurian Romance: A Short Introduction* (Blackwell, 2003)

Filmsand TV

The Adventures of Sir Lancelot (TV, 1956–57)
Camelot (movie, 1967)
Camelot (TV, 2011)
Les Chevaliers de la Table Ronde (movie, 1990)
Excalibur (movie, 1981)
First Knight (movie, 1995)
Gawain and the Green Knight (movie, 1973)
Knights of the Round Table (movie, 1953)
Lancelot and Guinevere (movie, 1963)
Lancelot du Lac (movie, 1974)
Legend of Prince Valiant (TV, 1991–94)
Magic Sword: The Quest for Camelot (movie, 1998)
Perceval le Gallois (movie, 1978)
Prince Valiant (movie, 1954)
Tristan and Isolde (movie, 2006)